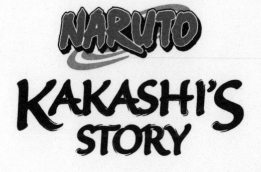

NARUTO
KAKASHI'S STORY

Masashi Kishimoto
Akira Higashiyama

NARUTO KAKASHI-HIDEN HYOTEN NO IKAZUCHI
© 2015 by Masashi Kishimoto, Akira Higashiyama
All rights reserved.
First published in Japan in 2015 by SHUEISHA Inc., Tokyo.
English translation rights arranged by SHUEISHA Inc.

Cover and interior design by Shawn Carrico

Translation by Jocelyne Allen

Published by
VIZ Media, LLC
P.O. Box 77010
San Francisco, CA 94107

www.viz.com

Kishimoto, Masashi, 1974-
  [Naruto. Kakashi Hiden: Hyouten no Ikazuchi. English]
  Naruto: Kakashi's story : lightning in the frozen sky / Masashi Kishimoto, Akira Higashiyama ;
translated by Jocelyne Allen.
     pages cm. -- (Naruto)
  ISBN 978-1-4215-8440-9 (paperback)
  1. Ninja--Fiction. I. Higashiyama, Akira, 1937- II. Allen, Jocelyne, 1974- translator. III. Title. IV.
Title: Kakashi's story : Lightning in the frozen sky. V. Title: Lightning in the frozen sky.
  PL872.5.I57N3413 2015
  895.6'36--dc23
                          2015028431

Printed in the U.S.A.

First printing, November 2015

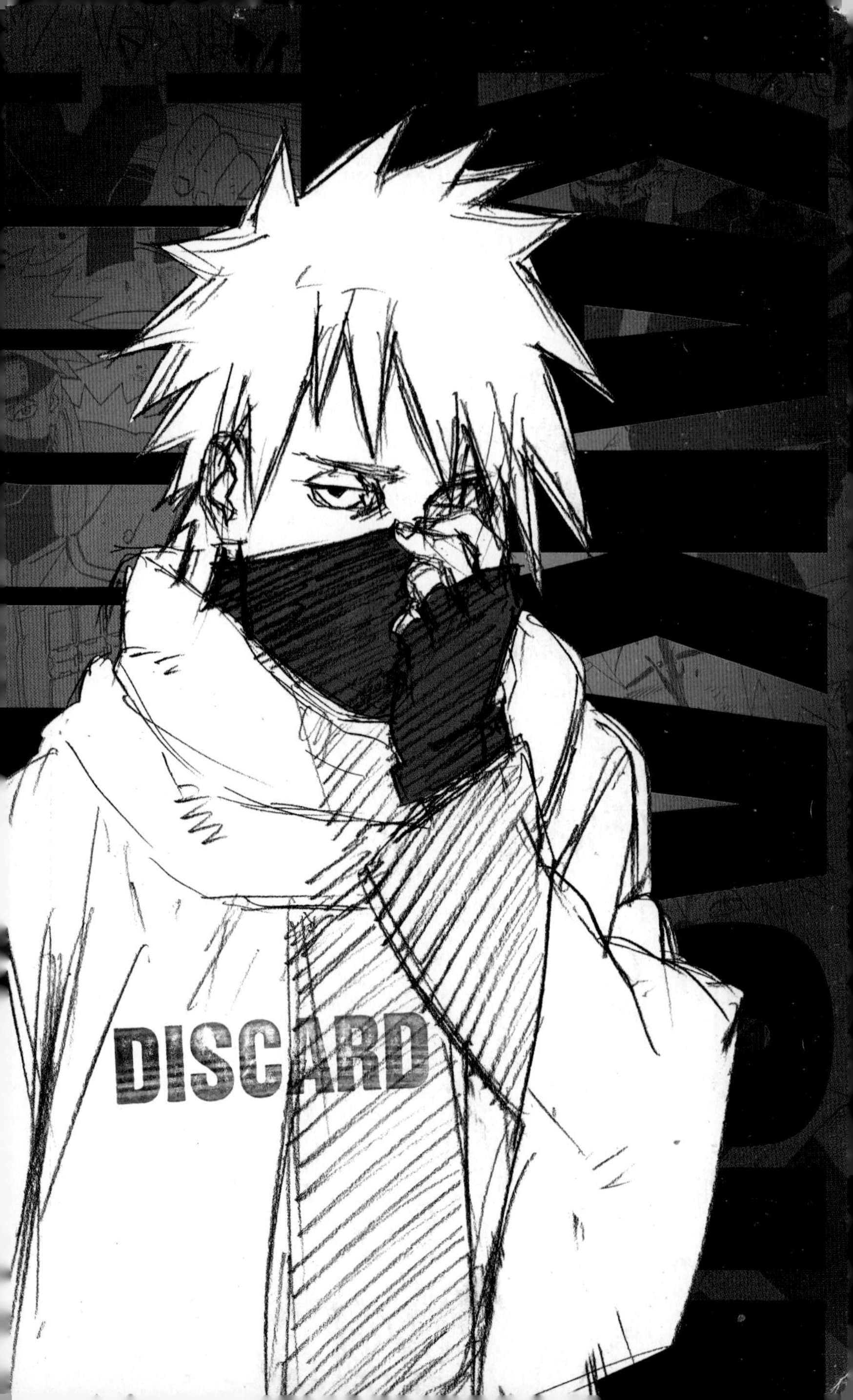

六代目火影

KAKASHI'S STORY

Lightning in the Frozen Sky

ORIGINAL STORY BY
Masashi Kishimoto

WRITTEN BY
Akira Higashiyama

TRANSLATED BY
Jocelyne Allen

Lightning
in the

CONTENTS

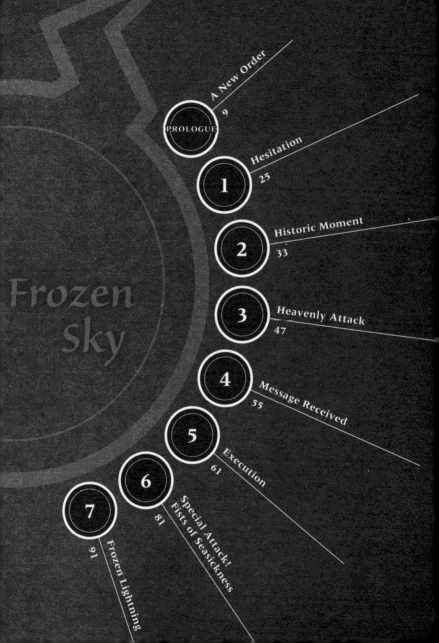

Frozen Sky

CHARACTERS

はたけカカシ
Ninja from Konohagakure
HATAKE KAKASHI

うずまきナルト
Ninja from Konohagakure
UZUMAKI NARUTO

マイト・ガイ
Ninja from Konohagakure
MIGHT GUY

華氷
(かひょう)
Ninja of the Ryuha Armed Alliance
KAHYO

羅氷
(らひょう)
Ninja of the Ryuha Armed Alliance
RAHYO

我龍
(がりょう)
Head of the Ryuha Armed Alliance
GARYO

PROLOGUE

A New Order

A New Order

Five hundred meters above the ground, with a strong wind pushing up against him, Sai looked back over his shoulder.

"You sure you're going to be okay alone, Naruto?"

"Yeah." Naruto glared at the enemy territory far below him. "No problem."

"But your hand's still—"

"I can take these guys with one hand."

The Chinese phoenix, created with the Art of Cartoon Beast Mimicry, slipped through the shadows of the night, invisible from the ground. However, Naruto's eyes could make out that ground quite clearly.

It was past midnight, but the torches of the night watch still burned brightly in the wild mountain valley where his target hid away from him. Here and there, ninjas stood watch. Bathed in the cold light of the moon, the sharply rising stone wall and the needlelike ridgeline glistened as if wet.

"A stronghold with natural defenses." Sai voiced Naruto's own thoughts. "So Garyo's been running around and hiding in places like this, huh?"

"While he kills the people of the Land of Waves." Naruto gritted his teeth.

It was a September night, a year after the end of the Fourth Great Ninja War. The powerful wind howled as it ripped through the valley.

Shifting positions, the giant bird carrying Sai and Naruto made a wide turn, and they caught sight of Garyo's base directly below.

"Don't think too hard about it, Naruto. It's not like the Fourth Great Ninja War's going to be the last war humanity fights. As much as I hate it, we're still going to see people who sympathize with Madara's thinking," Sai told him, before Naruto jumped down from the large bird.

"Like Garyo, y'know?"

Krrrrrrrr!

Listening to the sound of his own body tearing through the air, Naruto intertwined the index and middle fingers of his left hand to make a cross and dropped down into the night sky. He had learned this new way of weaving signs after losing his right arm in the fight with Sasuke.

"Multiple Shadow Doppelgangers!"

Bomf! White smoke surged up, and by the time the night watch noticed anything, Garyo's hideout was already surrounded by shadow doppelgangers.

"Enemy attack!" Angry voices sprang forth from the darkness here and there.

"Protect Garyo!"

Enemy ninja came flying out of huts arrayed along the stone wall and from the caves all around. Naruto's shadow doppelgängers launched kunai in all directions, and several members of the enemy group fell at once. Faced with slashing attacks from behind, Naruto turned into a cloud of smoke and disappeared.

The base's central plaza was instantly transformed into a battlefield with ninjas exchanging angry roars.

Naruto's vision swept both sides, searching for the cave Kakashi had told him about—a cave with two pointed rocks like fangs hanging from the ceiling, the sole entrance to Garyo's hideout, cut off from the outside world by the mountains. Or so Kakashi had said.

"So then, if he's thinking about escaping, he'll run straight to that cave!"

He could see it beyond the shadow doppelgangers performing their dance to the death with the enemy. The cavern, the mouth of a rock beast with fangs bared, was guarded by ninja, and the small man running inside, the hem of his long garment dragging, was—

"Garyooooo!" Naruto's voice echoed off the stone walls. "You're not going anywhere!"

Before the lingering echoes of Naruto's voice had dissipated, a single enemy ninja appeared to block his way. The ninja's costume was white like snow; the ninja's face was hidden under a white mask in the shape of a hook.

"Get out of my way!" Naruto didn't hesitate to launch several kunai.

But the instant the tips of the knives touched the masked ninja, their target shimmered and disappeared like mist. What was worse, before Naruto knew it, that very ninja had taken up a position behind him.

"Ice Style! Chains of Earthen Ice!"

He felt the jutsu hit his back lightly. He pitched forward the tiniest bit, but kept his balance. He braced himself and whirled around, kunai glittering as they sped toward the masked ninja— or rather, he fully intended to have them glitter and speed.

But he couldn't throw them.

"W-what is this...?"

The sensation of reeling within his body was in the next instant transformed into intense pain.

Snap, crack...krrk krrk krrk krrk!

Countless frozen thorns sprang up from his veins and ripped through his body.

"Unnnnh..." A puff of white breath slipped out of his mouth as he fell to his knees. However cool the mountains at night might have been, it was still only September. Yet Naruto's teeth were chattering, and his entire body was assaulted by a ferocious cold.

The ice quickly spread out from where the masked ninja had hit his back to every part of his body. The frost crawling across him wrapped itself around his arms and legs before creeping toward his face.

Krrk krrk krrk krrk krrk krrk krrk krrk!

He tried to get his body to move somehow, but only caused several thin pieces of ice to crackle as they peeled off and fell to the ground. The ice chains held Naruto firmly.

Not even sparing a glance for the frozen Naruto, the masked ninja returned to Garyo. "Lord Garyo, please, this way."

But Garyo didn't move, and the three ninja protecting him collapsed noisily in a pile of arms and legs.

Stunned beneath the hook-patterned mask, his enemy's eyes scrutinized the scene.

A hand gripping a kunai slowly appeared from the darkness behind Garyo. "Y'know, Haku wore a mask like that too." Naruto plunged a kunai into the neck of his target. "And now this ice technique... You a rogue ninja from Kirigakure?"

"So, that wasn't the real you." The masked ninja glanced back at the Naruto dispatched only seconds earlier. "I did think your response was not quite up to par for *the* Uzumaki Naruto, the man who defeated our Madara."

The doppelganger imprisoned by ice disappeared with a pop. The ice that had bound it cracked and scattered all at once. Naruto and his opponent met each other's eyes.

"I'll be taking Garyo back."

"Can't help you out there," the ninja said.

Naruto glared at the masked ninja. "'Cause of you guys, hundreds of people in the Land of Waves died."

"For an ideal."

"Madara's ideal? In the war, that was already—"

"Uchiha Madara's failure," Garyo interrupted Naruto, "was the fact that he attempted to cast Infinite Tsukiyomi on the entire world."

Naruto looked down on the small, dark man he had stabbed with a kunai. The unwavering ambition shrouding his entire body seemed completely unaffected by the point of the kunai being pressed into his neck. His long white hair was pulled back in a single bun, and a white beard grew from his chin. One of his long, almond eyes was clouded white.

"But Madara's thinking was not, in and of itself, incorrect," Garyo continued, the long hem of his garment fluttering in the wind. "To rid the world of war and realize ultimate justice, there is only the Infinite Tsukiyomi. It is true that Madara is dead. And the Infinite Tsukiyomi was also consigned to eternal oblivion by Uchiha Sasuke. However, that said, his ideal must not die. We may be forced to other methods, but we will approach Madara's ideal step by step. I truly believe this."

"Just what are you planning to do?"

"What is ultimate justice? It is the equality of all people. All unhappiness in this world arises from inequality. So then what should we do to realize this equality? We must control the freedom of the individual. The freedom to earn money, the freedom to possess more than others, the freedom to have it easier than others—I fight to control freedoms like these. And if our experiments go well, other lands will endorse us and our ideals. All freedoms in this world will be controlled. *This* is the true meaning of Madara's ideal, a new world order."

"So you picked the Land of Waves as the place for your experiments." Naruto pushed his voice out from between clenched teeth. "There are no hidden villages in this land, you know. Killing people who don't know the first thing about fighting... You're the ones who brought hatred and sadness into this country. It used to be a peaceful place."

"As long as there is inequality in this world, no country is without hatred and sadness."

A sudden gust blew into the cave, and Naruto's empty right sleeve flapped.

"There is no hidden village in this country. Thus, many rogue ninja come to live here. The rogue ninja who come to the Land of Waves have grown tired of killing each other. They hide the fact that they are ninja and try to live as normal people. What they want is a modest, humane life. But they have learned nothing but how to kill each other from childhood; what else can they do? The people of the Land of Waves despise them and think they can buy their dignity with money. They think that when they need military power, they can simply pay to hire someone like you. They think everything can be resolved with money, that they need never dirty their own hands. Money! Money! Money! Those without money are not even treated like human beings. The one you fought just now is one such unfortunate."

Naruto cast his eyes toward the masked ninja.

"This ninja's son was stung by a giant hornet and brought to hospital, but there was no doctor there. Nor at the next hospital, or the one after that; not a doctor to be found in the land. When some shady witch doctor was finally tracked down—a man who could hardly be called a doctor—the boy was in shock and on the verge of dying. Naturally, the spells and all the rest were of no use at all. If that poor lad had gotten treatment right away, perhaps they could have saved him. But every last doctor had disappeared from the Land of Waves. Why do you think that is?" Garyo caught himself before squeezing out in a suffering tone, "Because they had all been bought by the five great countries to attend to wounded ninja troops during the Fourth Great Ninja War."

Naruto's eyebrows leapt up.

"If the Land of Waves is at peace, then it is a peace built out of a pile of banknotes seized by stomping on these impoverished people," Garyo said. "Can you really say that there is no hatred or sadness in this land?"

He had no reply.

The masked ninja spoke instead. Quickly crouching down, Naruto's opponent hit the surface of the earth with the palm of one hand. "Ice Style! Chains of Earthen Ice!"

"What?!"

The shock wave rumbled in his stomach as it raced forward, splitting the ground. Countless icicles sprouted from below and spread out in the cave, piercing the ceiling but carefully avoiding where Naruto and Garyo stood. In the blink of an eye, his escape route had been blocked off.

"So long as there is a hint of moisture in the air, I can freeze anything with my Earth Chain Ice." The ninja's voice was low and hoarse through the mask. "And now, you have nowhere to go... Hand Garyo over."

Enemy ninja steadily gathered around them.

"I feel sorry for your son."

A moment of silence passed.

"But I just can't get on board with what you guys are doing," Naruto said. "You kill people who won't give up their freedom, and that's supposed to make everyone left happy? All that's gonna do is breed new hatred."

"There is no revolution without pain," his enemy said from within the hook mask. "These are the birth pangs necessary to create a new order."

"There has to be some other way."

"You don't actually intend to debate this here."

Naruto didn't bother to answer.

"If you won't come to me, I'll have to make you."

"Sorry, but I'm not interested in fighting you," Naruto said. He wrapped an arm around Garyo, kicked at the ground, and flew upward.

"So you run!" A heartbeat later, the masked ninja also danced up into space, quickly moving deft fingers in tiny gestures. "Ice Sword!"

A sound like shattering glass echoed through the mountains. The water in the air condensed to become countless daggers of ice, all headed straight for Naruto. The tips glittered under the light of the moon.

But Naruto was the one grinning.

The ice swords were about to carve through him when a black whirlwind abruptly snatched Naruto and Garyo away. Slicing through empty air, the ice swords plunged into the stone wall.

Skreeee! A bird's cry reverberated in the ravine.

Landing, the masked ninja looked up with white-hot eyes as Garyo was whisked away by the black bird.

"Nice timing!"

"That went well, huh?"

On the back of the enormous phoenix, Naruto and Sai slapped the palms of their hands together.

∞

"It's already been six years since then, huh? So then that means I was still twelve! That was our first job as Team Seven. Kakashi was there, Sakura was there, even Sasuke was there."

"Only six years," Inari corrected Naruto. He was supposedly fourteen, but he had a much more adult air to him than Naruto. A leather tool bag hung from his hip, filled with hammers and saws and other implements. "In just six years, the Land of Waves has completely changed. Naruto, you've noticed it, right? I mean, you..."

"Are you talking about this right hand of mine?"

Inari looked away. In the fight with Sasuke, Naruto had lost his right arm above the elbow.

"Thing like this, it's no big deal!" Naruto opened his mouth wide and laughed heartily. "I got something way more precious than an arm."

"...Is it always going to be like that?"

"Right now, Auntie Tsunade's making me a prosthetic. So don't worry, Inari."

"She is...?"

"What's more important is, how're things in the Land of Waves?"

"That time... The time I first met you, me and Grandpa and everyone, we all believed we'd be happy as long as we could build the Great Naruto Bridge," Inari said, flashing a sad smile. "But thanks to the bridge, we got more traffic, sales got better, and more people got rich. So then everyone ended up totally focused on money. I mean, it's not unusual at all now to see guys who'll do anything for money, like Gato."

"Before, when I saw you just for a minute, that was...?"

"When we went to repair the damage Pain did to Konohagakure."

"We didn't get a chance to really talk then. Huh, so that's what the Land of Waves is like now?"

In the silence, Naruto looked down on the grave markers of Momochi Zabuza and Haku nestled against each other. The rough markers, simple pieces of wood in the shape of a cross, did indeed have the days and nights of six years carved into them. Kakashi had thrust the Executioner's Blade into the ground next to Zabuza's grave, only for it to be carried off by Sasuke's companion Suigetsu.

The wind cut through the grassy field, causing the indigenous cosmos flowers to shudder.

Naruto stretched with a grunt. "Reminds me, how's old man Tazuna? He doing okay?"

After hesitating slightly, Inari blurted out, "He's been holed up in the shipbuilder's at the port, putting the finishing touches on Tobishachimaru."

"Is he making a new ship?"

"Yes, but one that flies."

"Huh?"

"The Land of Waves right now is trying to build a new transport system. Once the Tobishachimaru is complete, the Land of Waves will become the number one transport hub in the world. Using air routes, we'll be able to deliver in a few hours packages that right now take boats or people several days to transport." Inari's tone was, in contrast to the tale of economic prosperity he was telling, somehow cold with a hint of self-derision. "It's actually still a secret, but I think it's okay for me to tell you, Naruto. Once the first ship is complete, there's going to be an unveiling and a sightseeing trip with all the most important people in the Land of Waves invited. To show everyone the marvel that is the Tobishachimaru and get more money, you know? And once they collect more money, they're going to just keep building new ships and then sell them to the five major nations. And this is still a secret too, but my grandpa and them said Konohagakure was asked to do security during the sightseeing flight."

"I know some shinobi can fly, but...can they really make a boat that flies?"

"Well, while the five great nations were spending all their time in war, the Land of Waves continued to develop new technologies."

"Is the ship big?"

"I think the one Grandpa and them are building now can hold about fifty or sixty people. If they just had the money, they could make something much bigger."

"So just how are they gonna make a big boat like that fly?"

"You can just think of it as a big balloon," Inari said. "They fill this balloon with a gas that's lighter than air, and then below it, there's an iron basket that holds people and things. It's called a gondola; it's attached to the underside of the balloon. At the tail of the boat, there are six propellers used to push the ship through the air."

What popped into Naruto's mind was the image of a bamboo basket with many tiny balloons attached to it. He got to it floating in the air without any issues, but then a large flock of crows came flying out of nowhere and popped the balloons with many loud bangs. And then the people tumbled out of the bamboo basket and fell upside down straight down into hell.

"No way I'm stepping into anything like that!" A shudder ran through his entire body. "Inviting all the bigwigs—you sure it's really safe?"

"They're doing a million test flights."

"So? You're not into it, Inari?"

"...Huh?"

"It's written all over your face." Naruto shrugged. "That the truth is you could live without a boat that flies."

"...Yeah." Inari dropped his eyes. "It's true that there'll be lots of money coming into the Land of Waves once they finish the Tobishachimaru."

"And you're not so keen on that?"

"It's fine."

Naruto raised a skeptical eyebrow.

"But I think a lot of people'll show up to work on it." Inari raised his head and looked directly at Naruto. "Right from the start, our Land of Waves has made its living via transport.

The people who have carried the burden of those commodities on their shoulders, the people who have carried them in ships, they'll probably all be out of work. And then what happens? Everyone starts to hate the Tobishachimaru. They start to hate us, the carpenters, who built a thing like this."

Money! Money! Money! Garyo's voice sprang to life in Naruto's ears. *If the Land of the Waves is at peace, then it is a peace built out of a pile of banknotes seized by stomping on these impoverished people.*

Seeing Naruto's serious face, Inari changed the subject. "By the way, thanks for catching Garyo. His gang was against building the Tobishachimaru right from the start. They attacked the carpenters I don't know how many times; they even killed some people. So Garyo was sent to Hozuki Castle?"

"Yeah, probably."

Hozuki Castle was a containment facility for prisoners, built in Kusagakure and paid for by the five principal territories. Naturally, all five managed it cooperatively.

Several years earlier, Naruto had been charged with a certain mission and infiltrated Hozuki Castle. In the events of that time, the castle had been completely destroyed, and he knew that it was Inari and the carpenters of the Land of Waves who had repaired it.

"Speaking of that, you got tossed into Hozuki Castle once, right, Naruto? You peeked into the ladies' bath, huh?"

"I'm telling you that was my mission!"

Inari took one look at Naruto and his bulging eyes and laughed.

His laughter was infectious, and Naruto joined in. "Well, anyway, the world just keeps changing, you know?" He kept talking, grinning. "Money's just like kunai or ninjutsu: it's good or bad depending on how you use it, maybe."

Inari nodded.

"You use that money the right way, and you'll probably help out a ton of people," Naruto said. "I don't really know, but I figure that's maybe the best way to fight back against guys like Garyo."

CHAPTER 1

Hesitation

CHAPTER 1

Hesitation

Just like every other time, Naruto flew out of Ichiraku holding a bowl of ramen. "Master Kakashi! Master Kakashi!"

Kakashi had absolutely no desire to see Naruto. He pretended to be totally absorbed in the book he had just picked up—his favorite, *Make-Out Tactics*, and in particular the riveting third chapter "Shut up and Follow Me," which had the highest level of make-outedness in the entire series—and tried to wait out the storm. And yet Naruto had almost no concept of other people's feelings.

"Master Kakashi! Come on, I've been calling your name for ages now, you know. You're not old enough to be going deaf yet."

"Hm? Oh, Naruto." Kakashi sighed in his heart. "Sorry, excuse me. I was completely immersed in this book, I didn't realize. Oh! Your prosthetic arm's finished?"

"Yeah, but I still haven't got the hang of it yet," he said, clumsily opening and closing the chopsticks he held in his right hand. "Well, guess I can't really complain."

"I guess not."

"Anyway, Master Kakashi, you still haven't undertaken the inauguration ceremony?"

"What?" *See? Here we go.* "Hmm, well, I'm not too good at that sort of thing."

Lately, wherever he went, someone was asking him this question. Kakashi was a little disconcerted by it.

He had indeed resolved to become the Hokage. But he personally thought he wasn't the Hokage vessel, after all. If he went through with the inauguration ceremony, he really wouldn't be able to turn back. He even thought from time to time that now that the Fourth Great Ninja War was at an end, there was no real need to be in such a rush to be the Hokage.

"The Hokage Monument's already done, you know." Naruto clumsily used his new right hand to shovel ramen noodles into his mouth between sentences. "I mean, everyone's kinda concerned here. First off, if we don't make it totally clear who the Hokage is, we won't have any control over the other villages. That's what the ceremony's for, right?"

"Lady Tsunade is still very much in good health, so I don't really—"

"Granny Tsunade's already done, I'm telling you," Naruto dared to state what loomed large. "Ever since she almost died in the war before, she hasn't been putting herself into her work, you know?"

"...She hasn't?"

"She starts drinking in the middle of the day, and just when you notice she's suddenly gone, she's getting into a huge fight at some gambling den. It's maybe, like, in that war, she got a real feel for the fact that she's old, you think?" Naruto laughed heartily. "And I mean, if you gotta go, go big, right?"

But Kakashi was in no position to laugh along with his student. He had detected no ordinary black bloodlust coming from behind Naruto, but rather a huge and boiling wave of wrath.

"But, you know, Granny Tsunade's getting up there. Makes sense that she wants to retire already and enjoy her golden years."

"Uh, umm, is that so?" The bloodlust lurking just over Naruto's shoulder, growing ever more intense, flustered Kakashi. "I think Lady Tsunade is still very young, yes, that is exactly what I think!"

"How?! Maybe you can't tell from far away, but when you look at her up close, her face is just covered in tiny wrinkles."

"Aaah!" *I'm begging you, shut your mouth already!* "You! Don't say things like that so loudly."

Each time Naruto tossed off one of these remarks, the bloodlust growled and became even greater.

"What're you getting so upset about, Master Kakashi?" Naruto was oblivious to the pair of glittering eyes shining behind him. "I won't say it too loud, but lately, she's been in some kind of temper. And she forgets stuff everywhere."

He's dead.

Kakashi closed his eyes, so he didn't see Tsunade sink her clenched fist into Naruto's head. However, he couldn't stop the very unfunny sound of the sharp crack from reaching his ears.

"Just who is forgetting things everywhere?" Tsunade's angry roar rang out. "And the reason I'm in a temper is because you are always making me angry!"

Closing his eyes, an enormous bump growing on his head, Naruto prostrated himself on the ground.

"Kakashi!"

"Y-yes ma'am!" With Tsunade glaring fiercely at him, Kakashi's voice was turned inside out. "I-I was just saying you're plenty young, Lady—"

"Have you still not decided on a day for the inauguration?"

Kakashi averted his eyes.

"I well understand your hesitation." Tsunade's face softened. "I was like that too."

"You were...?"

"Once you become Hokage, you can no longer live in your own way as you have to this point." She indicated the prostrate Naruto with her chin. "You won't be able to spend much time with this idiot anymore, either."

Kakashi stayed silent and listened.

"You are the only one who can be the sixth," Tsunade said. "Naruto has indeed grown stronger, but as you can see, he is still not a vessel for the Hokage. And at the time of the Five Kage Summit, you were firm in your resolve to become Hokage, were you not?"

"At the time, I still had the sharingan eye. But losing the sharingan means that I lost the Lightning Blade. Lightning Blade was a jutsu I could complete precisely because I had the dynamic vision of the sharingan. And I thought that with such a jutsu, I'd be able to protect Konoha somehow if I became Hokage."

"Kakashi..."

"I'm sorry, Lady Tsunade. Please wait to discuss this until your current term is finished."

"You must be the sixth Hokage, Kakashi." Obito's voice came back to life in his ears. *And then Obito gave me the sharingan.*

What am I hesitating for? Kakashi admonished himself. *Right from the start, the sharingan was a loan with an expiration date, wasn't it? Aah, I probably relied on it too much.*

"You were guarding the Tobishachimaru." Tsunade changed the subject. "Were there enough people on hand?"

"Just barely. This year, it's our turn with Hozuki Castle, so Team Guy and Shikamaru's Team Ten are going all out there."

"Hozuki Castle... I do wish a new castle master would be decided on soon."

"It's not going to be that easy to find a master on Mui's level."

In the joint tactical operation some years earlier carried out by Konohagakure and Kumogakure, Hozuki Castle had been destroyed. Although the castle itself had since been rebuilt, the castle master Mui, who controlled the prisoners using a technique called Celestial Prison, had lost his life. Ever since, Konoha, Suna, Kumo, Iwa, and Kiri had deployed guards in rotating months-long shifts.

"We need Naruto here protecting the village, so I'll take a group of jonin with me. It's just a ceremonial guard, though; there shouldn't be any problems. Once the boat's up in the air, my role there is done anyway."

"That reminds me, Guy said he wants you to let him do that job. Surprising that he'd say something like that with that leg of his."

"Guy just wants to see a ship flying," Kakashi said. "He might be able to go out to the Land of Waves in his wheelchair on that."

"A boat that flies... Truly incredible. Right now, the existence of the Tobishachimaru is a secret from the other countries, but..."

"They'll find out about it soon enough. When they do, all the countries will likely get together and ask their hidden villages to try and steal Tobishachimaru's lighter-than-air technology from the Land of Waves."

In other words, Kakashi added in his heart. *For the right to the skies, shinobi would start to deceive and kill each other once again.*

31

CHAPTER 2

Historic Moment

CHAPTER 2

Historic Moment

Regardless of the fact that the sightseeing flight was meant to be a secret, the curtain was lifted at the height of a magnificent ceremony.

In the grassy field by the sea, decorative paper balls were split open and white doves flew free from them, a drum and fife band marched about, and confetti danced in the air. It went without saying that the guests of honor who were to ride the Tobishachimaru, and even the mere attendants who had been placed at their disposal, all expressed their respect for the historic moment and watched the ceremony in full dress.

Behind the brilliant men and women taking the stage one after another and offering congratulatory addresses stood the proud form of the enormous streamlined Tobishachimaru, 223 meters in total length, diameter of 34 meters, top speed of 70 kilometers per hour, the tail equipped with six thrust propellers. A gondola compartment was attached to the bottom of the massive body.

Tobishachimaru—the three characters of the name meant flying *shachi* boat, and the origin of this name was very clear. On the balloon, an enormous tiger-headed shachi carp had been carefully painted, right down to the dorsal and pectoral fins.

The weather was superb—there was not a cloud in the sky, and the cool wind of late autumn blew through the grasses to make rustling waves.

"It's the perfect day." Slight tears welled up in Tazuna's eyes as he gazed upon the ship he had had a hand in building. "Now the Land of Waves will be incredibly strong once more."

"Congratulations," Kakashi replied. "You've made something wonderful, Tazuna."

"Did you know? That huge balloon there's called an air bladder. Got helium gas inside it."

"Helium's lighter than air and not flammable, right?"

"Mm-hmm, that's Tobishachimaru's buoyancy right there. Look. There's six propellers on the tail there, right?"

Kakashi nodded.

"Those push that massive thing forward. This time's a sightseeing flight, two and a half hours, but we tweak things a bit and we should be able to achieve significantly longer flight ranges. Although, to keep other countries from learning about the ship, we have to stay at an altitude of five thousand meters or lower. As long as we don't go above five thousand meters on today's flight, we should be safe from the prying eyes of the intelligence services of the other nations. We checked it all out. And the reason the ship was painted that precise shade of light blue is to make it blend in with the color of the sky."

"But Konoha has been informed about it?"

"Well, there was no way around that." All smiles until that point, Tazuna's face clouded over. "All fine and good for Garyo to have been sent to Hozuki Castle, but his followers have infiltrated every level of society."

"That's exactly why we have the masters of Konoha concealed inside the ship."

"We're really counting on you."

"Now, let us at last proceed to board!" A proud voice echoed from the stage, urging the guests toward the ship. "Those lucky fifty-seven guests fortunate enough to have invitations, please make your way to the Tobishachimaru! The attendants will show you inside!"

"Finally, hmm?"

At Kakashi's words, Tazuna narrowed his eyes, overwhelmed with emotion. "Yes, finally making history here."

They looked out over the people, laughing and chatting in their finery, streaming toward the Tobishachimaru. The playing of the drum and fife band grew noticeably louder.

Kakashi heard hurried footsteps from behind just as the last guests stepped onto the ramp and the photo session to commemorate the occasion began.

"Wait!" A woman holding up the hem of a long blue dress came running at top speed. "I'm getting on! I'm getting on the ship as well!" Clutched in the hand she was waving wildly above her head was a gilded invitation.

Just as she was about to run past Kakashi, the woman tripped and pitched forward. "Waah!" she cried in a small voice as her body was thrown into the air.

Almost reflexively, Kakashi stopped her.

In the confusion, their eyes met. Flowing, curly hair, slightly parted lips, large, moist eyes open in surprise—time stopped for a moment, and the world, to Kakashi, was this woman and nothing else.

The woman in the long dress fell into Kakashi's arms, her hair softly tickling the end of his nose as she raised her head.

"Are you all right?"

"Oh! Excuse me." The woman hurriedly pulled herself upright. "I was in a bit of a hurry. Thank you so much for helping me in a moment of danger."

Kakashi nodded, and she avoided meeting his eyes, embarrassed. And then she lifted the hem of her dress once more and charged toward the Tobishachimaru, yelling loudly, "Wait! Please waaaiit! I'm getting on, I'm a passenger as well!"

"People are that excited to go on the sightseeing trip," Kakashi remarked to Tazuna, watching the woman running away from behind. "Carpentry is really a wonderful occupation."

"She's a real beautiful woman, too," Tazuna said. "And speaking of occupations, you still not having your big day?"

Again?

Kakashi shook his head ambiguously. His eyes were turned toward the Tobishachimaru waiting to take off as the woman in the long dress rushed to the gangplank.

"I don't really know, but isn't the Hokage inauguration ceremony kinda like a wedding between you and Konohagakure?"

"Yes," Kakashi answered absently, staring at the propellers on the tail. "I guess you could say that."

"Then it'd be strange not to have doubts. And all the more so with everyone expecting so much of you."

Kakashi looked closely at the gondola bathed in the morning light, casting a black shadow on the green grasses.

"For instance, suppose that beautiful woman just now was seriously chasing after you to marry her. No matter how beautiful she might be, a man's going to flinch at that."

"Mm-hmm." But Tazuna's voice was for the most part not reaching Kakashi's ears. "You don't say."

"When a woman's too aggressive, a man just pulls back. And this is exactly why when I was young, I went chasing round after tail like a starving dog—"

"Tazuna," Kakashi interrupted the other man. His eyes were firmly fixed on a suspicious man jumping down from the tail of the ship. "I might have just gotten called to work."

Leaving behind Tazuna, and the question mark floating over his head, Kakashi raced toward the Tobishachimaru.

The woman, who had just run up onto the gangplank, appeared to be the last passenger. The workers began releasing the ropes that affixed the ship to the earth. The sky-blue machine groaned quietly as it made its preparations to leave the ground.

"Hey!" Kakashi called from behind, and the man in the black, hooded cloak jumped and stood still. It was the man who had snuck down from the tail of the Tobishachimaru while he was talking with Tazuna. "You're not an invited guest, huh?"

The man started running.

"Stop!"

Kakashi took off in pursuit, only to receive a sharp kick that came flying out from under the hem of the man's cloak. Opening his stance, he dodged the enemy attack and threw out a number of his own attacks in succession.

One blow, two, three, the pair attacked each other. Kakashi could tell his opponent was quite masterful. He made no wasted movement.

But while they exchanged a fourth and fifth blow, he came to see through his enemy's tactics. No sooner had he thought that a kick would come at the same time as a thrust, his opponent launched that very attack. He read the show of tripping as actually moving in for a series of blows to his torso, and his enemy moved exactly as he anticipated; it was almost fun to watch.

Kakashi knew this attack pattern only too well. On top of

CHAPTER 2

that, he felt absolutely no bloodlust here, nor the minutest sense of any ninjutsu being activated. As if to confirm his suspicions, that back might have been covered in a black cloak, but—

Lowering his head and dodging a kick, Kakashi charged at his enemy.

He deftly handled the succession of lunges and dropped his hips to kick his enemy's feet out from under him as he shot out a rapid-fire five-blow combo using his fists and elbows.

Crack!

Whmp!

"Aaaaah!" Sent flying, the enemy fell to the ground, legs and arms spasming.

"My, my." Kakashi approached his opponent and pulled back the hood hiding his face. "The fact that you're here means that Guy's come too, hm?"

Below the hood was the face of an unconscious Rock Lee.

∞

Slipping through the crowd of onlookers and picture takers, Kakashi jumped up onto the last rope tying the Tobishachimaru to the ground.

He molded his chakra and swiftly climbed up with the power of his arms alone. Kicking with his legs to raise his body up, Kakashi took advantage of the centrifugal force and flew onto the body of the ship in a single leap.

He caught a glimpse of the passengers inside in their finery through the window of the gondola. Not one of them had noticed Kakashi passing by outside.

He lay facedown on the envelope—the side of the air bladder—then stood and ran up diagonally, heading for the tail as the crosswind pushed at him.

But, he thought. *That's some job with that body, avoiding the eyes of the jonin set up all over the ceremony grounds and sneaking onto the Tobishachimaru. Or maybe he bought off a jonin?*

Below the slowly ascending ship, the spectators gradually grew smaller and smaller.

Kakashi, having arrived at the tail of the ship, hung by one hand from the cover of the drive area. Inside were the propellers, about five meters each in diameter.

He probably got in through here. I have to get in there too before the propellers get going. He had this thought at almost the same time as the third propeller from the right started rotating.

Whk whk whk. With a low rumble, the propeller gradually picked up speed. The Tobishachimaru started to turn gently toward the right.

The air high up in the sky was much colder than he expected. The wind grew stronger as they gained altitude. Kakashi focused the chakra in his limbs and crawled along to the opposite side of the engine area so he wouldn't get buffeted by the wind.

When the ship stopped in the air for a moment, as if it had finally determined its route, the third propeller from the left appeared to be about to start spinning.

By the time Kakashi dove into the drive area, fighting the wind, the propeller had begun to spin slowly. After firmly planting his feet, he jumped headfirst through a gap in the rotating propeller. Fortunately, given that it wasn't rotating at top speed yet, he managed to make it through without his body bursting like an overripe tomato against the enormous blades.

But before he could even heave a sigh of relief, the

propeller had picked up speed to rotate with a great deal of force and threatened to suck him in.

"Ngh!"

Even using the chakra of his whole body and clinging to the interior of the drive area, the wind speed threatened to peel his body away and back into the propeller. Still, he inched forward and somehow managed to escape the engine area.

He looked around.

The route directly ahead of him was blocked by the buoyant air bladder, but there was a ladder that led to the engine area, and he used this to make his way down toward what seemed to be the engine room.

His ears picked up a strange sound. Shooting his gaze around the area, he spotted a person in a wheelchair, wearing the exact same black hood as Lee, racing along the scaffolding suspended above the engine room.

"You're not getting away from me!"

Kakashi leapt over the railing to drop down to the scaffolding. Even farther down seemed to be the ship's hold, and he could see several large wooden boxes piled up there.

The man in the wheelchair kept advancing, staggering somewhat, on the scaffolding running parallel to the beam upon which Kakashi stood.

Kakashi kicked off the scaffolding and leapt across the room to the other scaffold. "What are you up to, Guy!"

The wheelchair came to an abrupt stop.

"Lee spilled everything." Kakashi sighed and shook his head. "Honestly... You went so far as to tell him that if he didn't get you on the Tobishachimaru, you'd sever the apprentice-master bond?"

In the fight with Madara, Guy had shattered the bones in his right leg and been forced to use a wheelchair ever since. The doctor told him he'd never walk again.

But in a surprising turn, not only had he tirelessly bounced back from this adversity, but he had even recovered to the point of being able to stand and walk when he put forth the Full Power of Youth.

"Even without Lee, I can do whatever I want when I want to," Guy said. "With this body, I'm proof a person can live just fine without one or both legs."

"Now, look," Kakashi glanced at Guy's cast-covered right leg. "You went to the trouble of sneaking into the Tobishachi-maru just for that?"

"Get it, Kakashi? I'm not done as a shinobi quite yet. One, two thousand pistol squats with just my left leg are nothing. I might be in a wheelchair, but when I feel like it, getting into a boat like this is a piece of cake. Mwa ha ha ha!"

Kakashi simply stared with cool, half-closed eyes at the boundless optimism of the man before him.

"And I'll tell you right now, I didn't particularly want to get on this ship," Guy argued. "I had absolutely no interest in humanity's first flying ship or what have you. The scenery from five thousand meters up in the air? What good is looking at that going to do you? I don't even care how it's possible exactly for a boat that's two hundred twenty-three meters long and weighs over two hundred tons to fly anyway!"

Ah, come on, Kakashi thought. *You just really wanted to get on this thing.*

"W-what? What's with that look?"

"You know, you used to get terrible motion sickness."

"Unh!"

"What's wrong?" Kakashi couldn't suppress a sigh. "Let me tell you now. Don't go blaming me if you start throwing up or something."

"W-what?! Ridiculous! It might be a boat, but this one flies, doesn't it?"

"But a flying boat's still a boat."

"Quit with the condescension! As if I, Might Guy, would get sick on such a trifle as this!" But no sooner were the words out of his mouth than his face went pale, and he was struggling to hold down whatever was coming up from his stomach.

"Just what are you planning to do?" *Honestly. This is ridiculous.* "The shinobi concealed on this boat reported in advance to the Land of Waves. We didn't make any such report, and if we're found here like this, it'll damage the trust they have in Konoha. They might misunderstand our presence here and think we're trying to steal information about the Tobishachimaru."

"Not a problem."

"Huh?"

"This scenic flight is a secret from all the nations." Guy grinned. "Officially, the Tobishachimaru doesn't exist. You and I can't sneak into a boat that doesn't exist."

"Oh, I get it."

"I've accounted for everything! Mwa ha ha—Urp! Anyway, how's my favorite student?"

"If you're talking about Lee, I sent him to Hozuki Castle."

"You did? Well, Lee will be fine! With the Full Power of Youth I've ceded him, he'll watch carefully over the prisoners." Then he lowered his voice. "At any rate, I'm here with this body.

I can't do anything like supervise prisoners. So it's not a problem in the least for him to slip off for a little while."

"You... This is the total opposite of what you were saying before, isn't it?"

"What? We're not going to get caught! Anyway, to discuss things—Urp! Aah, I feel terrible... We're in here now, so how about you push my wheelchair and we take a spin around the place together?"

Here, Guy clamped his mouth shut and peered down towards the bottom of the ship's hold, his facial expression suddenly grim.

Kakashi had noticed it too.

"Ninja."

"Yeah." Kakashi nodded at Guy's statement. "There shouldn't be any ninja on this boat other than the ones above us."

The pair of men who had come into the ship's hold did not look like regular passengers. The way they moved without a sound, the sharp bloodlust turned outward, the gait that did not lose its balance even in the middle of this swaying ship; any one of these marked them as shinobi.

Kakashi and Guy tamped down their auras and watched the movements of the men below them. From above, they couldn't make out their faces. And their clothing was the same style as that of any other passenger.

The men didn't noticed Kakashi and Guy above them. They crouched down in a corner with wooden boxes piled high and did something before hurriedly leaving the area.

Kakashi and Guy exchanged looks.

Once the men were gone, Kakashi jumped down from the scaffolding and examined the area around the boxes. He soon found what he was looking for.

"Hey, Kakashi!" Guy called out, quietly.

"Did you find something?"

"Yeah," he replied, almost a groan. "Looks like things are about to get annoying."

It was a kunai with an explosive tag.

Immediately, there was a scream from the dining lounge.

CHAPTER 3

Heavenly Attack

CHAPTER 3

Heavenly Attack

"Come on! Can't you go any faster?! Aah, come on already. If my legs weren't out of action, I'd have already caught them by now and pounded all we needed to know out of them. Hurry up, Kakashi! The enemy's not going to stand around waiting for us, you know!"

"Seriously, you…" Kakashi pushed Guy's wheelchair and raced along the high scaffolding, cutting through the storehouse. The entire time, Guy had not been quiet for even a second.

"What's the matter, Kakashi? You're slowing down! Are you really a Konoha shinobi?!"

"You're really making me feel great here."

"And you! Get that hot blood of yours boiling! Then you naturally rescue others and can even save yourself. That's what'll make you feel great in the end, you know!"

This Might Guy doesn't understand sarcasm at all.

They abandoned the wheelchair in the galley, and after first pushing Guy up into the air duct, Kakashi jumped into the duct himself. They crawled along with Guy in the lead, pulling himself forward quickly with the strength of his arms alone.

Now that I'm thinking about it, this guy didn't just do left leg squats, he did push-ups like a maniac all day long, Kakashi thought, *watching the man in front of him. Honestly, your ridiculous stubbornness makes me feel better, Guy.*

When they came to the other side of the dining lounge ceiling, Guy stopped abruptly. And Kakashi slammed his face into Guy's butt.

"Don't stop so sudden—"

"Shh!" Guy beckoned Kakashi with a finger.

They looked down on the lounge through a vent cover set into the ceiling. Immediately to one side of the vent hung a large chandelier. In a corner of the lounge he could see a white grand piano, along with a neat arrangement of sofas and tables. There was even a bar serving alcohol by the windows.

"What are they doing?"

"Well," Kakashi replied, "it doesn't look like anything fun, does it?"

At that moment, several ninja were in the process of overpowering the passengers. They thrust kunai at them and showered them in jeers while they pushed and prodded the passengers all together in one place.

The baffled men and women, both young and old, were driven like sheep together into the center of the lounge. Small children clung to their mothers' waists and sobbed loudly. A man who complained was struck down by a shinobi.

"How many?" Kakashi asked, sharply.

"From where I sit, six—no, maybe seven?"

"Are the two from before there too?"

"Dunno." Now it was Guy doing the asking. "How many Konoha jonin are concealed aboard?"

"Three."

Before his voice had the chance to fade away, those jonin made their move.

One disguised as a passenger leapt away from the crowd and launched kunai at the enemy ninja with both hands. Two of the enemy collapsed to the floor.

Kakashi sent his eyes racing in the direction of a shriek to find another jonin crossing swords with the enemy directly under the luxurious chandelier hanging from the ceiling.

Perhaps they hadn't foreseen rebellion from the passengers; the enemy became overexcited. Several passengers fell because of some poorly aimed shuriken thrown by the enemy. An attacker's kick sent a jonin flying and crashing into some passengers, who tumbled to the floor.

"What are you doing?!" An enormous man in the center of the lounge howled. "What is Kahyo doing?!" He appeared to be the leader of the gang and wore chain mail over a navy ninja costume, beard covering the lower half of his face.

And then, Kahyo.

So that was the name of the woman who owned Kakashi's heart.

The third jonin jumped from the grand piano, clutching kunai in both hands, and sprang at this leader. The enemy drew a longsword he had hidden beneath his cloak to meet her challenge.

The fact that neither side carelessly activated any ninjutsu was likely because they were five thousand meters up in the air. If anyone made a wrong move and damaged the ship itself, it would be an invitation to catastrophe.

The kunai of the Konoha ninja and the leader of the attackers slammed against each other, sparks flying. The other two jonin were also facing off with enemies of their own.

"We gotta get in there and help, Kakashi!"

"With that body, what do you intend—Never mind. Just hold on a minute."

An unpleasant apprehension overwhelmed the urge he had to run in and support his fellow ninja. He soon understood why.

Kahyo.

Just as Konoha had slipped their own in amongst the passengers, the enemy apparently still had a trump card to be played.

This premonition of his was correct.

The first sign of it appeared around Guy's mouth. The voice urging Kakashi on expelled white mist. His breath was white. At the same time as Kakashi noticed this, he felt the precipitous drop in the cabin temperature. Returning his eyes to the battle in the lounge, he saw the movements of his ninja allies had stopped.

At first, he had no idea what was going on.

The three jonin also didn't seem to understand what was happening. They twisted their upper bodies desperately, but their lower halves didn't move an inch, almost as if they had been frozen solid.

Kakashi soon realized this was no metaphor. His compatriots were really frozen!

The thin ice snapped and crackled as it crawled upward on their bodies like a living creature. It quickly reached the tops of their heads, sealing the jonin in ice.

"W-what the..." Guy flapped his mouth open and closed, and the breath that came out was no longer white. "What's going on?"

"An enemy's mixed in with the passengers too." Kakashi felt the temperature rising on his skin. "And it looks like they're an Ice Style master."

"You got any ideas who it is?"

"That time two months ago when Naruto captured Garyo—"

Looking down on his frozen allies, Kakashi clenched his teeth tightly. "He said he faced an Ice Style master."

"So then, these guys are Garyo's lackeys?"

"Probably."

"So? What're we doing?"

"Hold on. They're moving."

"We are volunteers with the Ryuha Armed Alliance!" the large leader shouted. "All non-ninja passengers gather in the center of the room immediately!"

When he was finished, his underlings jabbed at the fearful, weeping passengers with kunai and herded them into the center of the dining lounge.

Another four or so newcomers came rushing into the lounge. Kakashi assumed the group had split into two groups to set up explosive tags within the ship.

The attackers deployed in pairs around the passengers and set up a monitoring system.

"Our demand is the immediate release of Lord Garyo, unjustly imprisoned at Hozuki Castle!" The leader roared thunderously. "If our demand is not met by precisely noon today, we will execute a passenger every ten minutes!"

Shrieks rose up from amongst the passengers.

"We know that Konohagakure serves as escort for this sightseeing tour! And we are well aware of the abilities of Uzumaki Naruto. If Konoha should attempt to use Uzumaki Naruto to regain control of this situation, you will be forever scorned as the village that abandoned these hostages to their deaths!"

Kakashi and Guy exchanged looks.

"We have already set up explosive tags in several places on this ship. If any one of us confirms the presence of Uzumaki

Naruto—even if we falsely confirm the presence of a bird that resembles Uzumaki Naruto—Tobishachimaru will explode in the sky and fall to earth as nothing but flaming cinders!"

By noon—thirty minutes left.

CHAPTER 4

Message Received

CHAPTER 4

Message Received

At 11:35 a.m., a letter attached to an arrow was shot into the wall of the Konohagakure Hokage office.

The demand on it was identical to the one the passengers on the Tobishachimaru had been forced to listen to five minutes earlier. The letter also clarified exactly how the attackers had snuck onto the ship.

In the Hokage office, Tsunade immediately moved to get confirmation of the situation—she contacted the Land of Waves with the wireless that had been introduced after the Fourth Great Ninja War and asked them to investigate the area noted in the letter.

There, twelve people were found stripped naked, hands and feet bound—the people originally invited to ride on the Tobishachimaru. They had been locked up in a small hut quite close to the plaza where the sightseeing flight ceremony had been held.

By the time all of this had been sorted out, they were down to twenty minutes before noon.

"In other words, the letter is not a joke," Tsunade announced to Shikamaru at Hozuki Castle after having Shizune align the frequencies. "Dammit! What are we supposed to do here?"

"Are we going to release Garyo?" Shikamaru asked forcefully over the wireless. "I don't know anything about this armed alliance or whatever it is, but if you give in to the demands of guys like this once, more people trying the same trick'll come out of the woodwork."

"Then what do you propose we do about the lives of the fifty-seven passengers on board?"

"Also, the other villages are not going to take it lying down if we go ahead and set a prisoner free because of our own problems."

"This is not the time for such talk!"

"P-p-please calm down, Lady Tsunade. At any rate, please make sure that Naruto at least does not find out about this. That idiot'll just charge in there by himself without thinking of anything past the end of his nose."

"Yes, I know."

Another voice came through Tsunade's wireless.

"Um, excuse me? Lady Tsunade? It's Lee."

"What is it, Lee?"

"Umm. The truth is, well..."

"What? If you have something to say, then simply say it!"

"Right. The truth is, Master Guy and Master Kakashi are on board the Tobishachimaru."

"What did you say?"

"Master Guy said he really wanted to ride on the ship. So I brought him there in secret today. Master Kakashi went after him... I'm sorry!"

"That Guy!" Tsunade's voice shook with anger. "I will murder him."

"You... Are you serious, Lee?" Shikamaru's gaze flew over to Ino. "Then that means—"

"Yup." Ino nodded. "I'll try contacting them via Mind Transmission."

Tsunade closed her eyes. Only the rustling sound of static

emitted by the wireless broke the silence.

"Shizune." Tsunade opened her eyes and ordered, "Get everyone in the village—everyone besides Naruto—together immediately."

CHAPTER 5

Execution

CHAPTER **5**

Execution

They had twenty minutes until the first execution.

Watching the enemy from inside the air duct for the last ten minutes, Kakashi had learned that their companions were also on standby on the ground and that this attack had already been communicated to Konohagakure.

And that wasn't all.

They had blown off the door to the pilothouse and gotten the pilots under their control as well.

"You the Hokage?" He could hear the leader's angry roar slipping out. "What's happening with Lord Garyo's release?!" Apparently, he had begun negotiating with Tsunade. "We can't wait that long! You have twenty minutes left. In twenty minutes, we do the first execution!"

He couldn't hear her reply.

"We are serious! If Lord Garyo is not released by noon, we will execute a passenger every ten minutes!" After this angry shout, the leader came out of the pilothouse and spoke to the passengers. "You heard what I said! Whether you live or die is on the head of Konohagakure!"

A shiver raced through the group of passengers shrunken and huddled together.

"What're we going to do, Kakashi?" Guy whispered sharply. "We bungle this, and they'll blow up the ship."

"We need to lower the ship's altitude somehow. This air

duct connects with the pilothouse, too. You should be able to get there if you keep crawling. Can I leave that to you?"

"What are you going to do? The first thing we need to do is collect all those explosive tag—Urp!"

"Ah! Idiot! At a time like this—"

Guy vomited magnificently, leading the attackers occupying the dining lounge to suspect that something was off.

"What was that, just now?!" Instantly, a huge commotion arose—a hornet's nest jabbed with a stick. "Urgh! What's that sour smell?!"

"The ceiling! Someone's hiding in the ceiling!"

At once, several kunai shot through the ceiling—*thk! thk! thk!*—grazing the tip of Kakashi's nose.

Kakashi and an ashen-faced Guy immediately fled to either side. In no time, lances were thrust into the ceiling, ripping Guy's cheek open.

"You okay, Guy?!"

"What, this little—Urp!"

Wait. That's not a lance. It's an icicle, an ice sword.

The ice sword ripped through the air duct and chased after them.

"Guy! You're in charge of the pilothouse!"

"L-leave it to me..."

They turned their backs on each other and crawled frantically through the air duct.

Kakashi had to twist his body up any number of times to avoid the ice swords. They just kept coming after him, like sharp fangs sprouting up from below. And they came to assault him from the front as well.

"Hngh!" He momentarily summoned his chakra to release a

jutsu. "Lightning Style! Violet Bolt!"

A pale purple tongue of lightning gushed from Kakashi's hand. *Zzzmp!* Together with the sound, the ice sword coming at him was vaporized and blown away.

Lightning Style, Violet Bolt. This was a new jutsu Kakashi had learned after losing his Lightning Blade.

In a narrow escape, an ice sword shredded the lingering afterimage of Kakashi fleeing through the hole in the air duct.

He had fallen into the washroom. By the time he grasped this, he was tangled up with a woman wearing a blue dress. Kakashi gently covered her mouth as she opened it to scream.

"Shh!"

"Mmmm!" The gagged woman struggled fiercely to try and get away from him somehow. "Mmmm... Mmmm!"

"I'm not going to hurt you!"

It was at that moment that he realized it was her. The long, flowing, curly hair, the large, wide-open eyes—they belonged to her, the woman still fresh in his memory.

"We met once before!" Kakashi told her. "You were about to fall and I caught you. Do you remember?"

And here it seemed the woman finally remembered who Kakashi was.

"I'm going to take my hand away. Can you stay quiet?"

The woman nodded with fearful eyes.

"I'm a shinobi from Konohagakure," Kakashi said as he released the woman's mouth. "I'm guarding this sightseeing flight. What are you doing in here?"

"I..." She got her breathing under control before replying. "I had just gone into the washroom when they attacked."

"And so you stayed hidden like this?"

The woman nodded again.

In the small washroom, they were standing with their bodies very nearly pressed up against each other. A faint scent of lavender drifted up to Kakashi's nose.

"At any rate, it'd be better to get out of here."

He looked up at the hole in the ceiling of the washroom, but the ice sword had disappeared without a trace. The user had released the jutsu.

Did Guy manage to escape okay?

"We'll go out through this hole." Kakashi flashed a smile at the reluctant woman to reassure her. "It's fine. We'll come out in the kitchen next door soon enough."

The woman blinked eyes wide with surprise.

"What's wrong?"

"Oh, no..." She hurriedly looked away. "Let's go."

So Kakashi lifted her up and pushed her into the air duct, and then followed after her himself.

They crawled along, and in no time at all they were dropping down into the kitchen through the opening he and Guy had used to climb into the ducts. Guy's wheelchair was still there, right where it had landed when they tossed it aside.

The woman started to say something, but Kakashi held her back, suddenly bit his thumb, and pressed her to the floor.

"Shinobi Conjuration!"

Poof! White smoke surged up, and eight ninja hounds appeared—Pakkun, Buru, Urushi, Guruko, Shiba, Biscuit, Uhei, and Akino.

"W-what?" The woman's eyes widened. "What are these dogs?"

"Where are we?" Buru shouted. "Oh, if it isn't Kakashi! Been a while!"

"Shh!" Kakashi held his index finger up to his mouth. "You're always so loud, Buru."

"Seeing you looking all gloomy like this..." Akino grinned from behind sunglasses. "Looks like you're still hesitating about formally becoming the Hokage, huh, Kakashi?"

"Sorry for being gloomy." *Even dogs are getting on my case.* "Anyway, to get right to it, I need your help."

"What's up, Kakashi?" Pakkun asked. "It's not like you to be in such a hurry."

"I don't have time to explain everything. Right now, you guys are five thousand meters above the ground."

The faces of the dogs all tightened up immediately.

"Explosive tags have been set up all over this ship," Kakashi added, rapid-fire. "I need you to find all of them without the enemy noticing."

"Got it!"

With Pakkun in the lead, the dogs flew out of the room.

"You hide here," he told the woman as he went to return to the air vents once more.

She grabbed on to his jacket. "What are you going to do?"

"They're going to start executing people in just a little bit," Kakashi said. "I have to stop them."

"They're demanding Garyo's release, right?"

"Uh..."

"Even hiding in the washroom, I could hear that raspy voice of his."

Kakashi nodded.

"Then all you have to do is release Garyo," the woman said, almost clinging to him. "The longer you all hesitate, the more victims there will be."

"We can't do that."

"Why not?"

"If we do what that lot says even just once, order will collapse."

"Order?" The woman laughed through her nose. "You all were at war a mere year ago, and now you talk about order?"

He simply stared at her.

"I'm sorry." The woman lowered her eyes. "But anyone who talks about a world of order usually thinks that they're the ones who are right, on the side of justice. War happens when two rights clash. And history only recognizes the rightness of the winner. Which is to say that the one with the most power is always right."

"I understand what you're trying to say. I mean, the Ryuha Armed Alliance is right in their own way."

"So then..."

"Even so, we can't release Garyo."

"Even if it means the lives of every passenger on board?"

"I am definitely not going to let that happen—or at least," Kakashi shrugged, "it would be so great if I could actually say that."

Now it was her turn to stay silent.

"I'll probably end up making some people victims myself. But I still want to save as many of the lives before me as I can."

The woman's eyes teared up, and her lips trembled.

"When two rights clash, the most important thing is to risk your life and put yourself in your opponent's position," Kakashi said, before he jumped back into the ducts. "Anyone who would easily take the lives of innocent bystanders in order to have their own words recognized has no right to talk about justice."

Kakashi crawled back through the ducts, punched the vent cover out, and dropped down into the dining lounge.

Thud!

The ninja of the Ryuha Armed Alliance were completely unsettled by the shinobi appearing from the ceiling. Several pulled out kunai and charged toward Kakashi.

He crouched down, and as he knocked aside enemy kunai with his arms, he shot out quick blows in succession. As soon as he sent one flying, he launched a kick at the next one, and without pausing to take a breath, he sent his barrage at a third.

In the blink of an eye, three enemies had fallen at his feet.

"Quit fooling around already!" The remaining enemies came at him with bloodshot eyes. "Come at me all at once!"

"Stop!" came the leader's angry roar.

The enemy ninja stopped moving.

"Back to your positions! Don't forget you're responsible for watching over the hostages. That's the copy ninja Hatake Kakashi. You're no match for him even in a group."

Kakashi sent his eyes racing around the room. Nine people, including the ones that had fallen. That was the number of the enemy as far as his eyes could see.

The passengers in a huddle in the center of the lounge watched how this would play out with looks of both fear and hope.

"The copy ninja Kakashi, hm?" The leader grinned. "Although now that you've lost the sharingan, I guess you're just plain old Kakashi."

"Well, even plain old Kakashi has some tricks up his sleeve."

"Like what?"

"Like chasing off vermin like you guys."

"So you say."

"Enough talk," Kakashi said. "Konoha does not negotiate with outlaws like you."

"I wonder." A daring smile spread across the enemy's lips, and he casually selected a passenger, pointing.

That was all.

"Aah…aah, th-that's…" The body of the selected passenger was enclosed in ice before their eyes. "W-what's this? What's happening?"

"?!"

The man, with a look of terror plastered on his face, was frozen.

"Aaaaaah!"

Screams rose up from among the passengers. They collapsed as if trying to get just a little farther away from the leader of the Ryuha Armed Alliance.

"So you still won't negotiate with us?"

"Stop it!" Kakashi shouted like he was spitting blood, but to this man, with a dull light shining in both eyes, the cry was like a heart-pleasing compliment.

Closing his eyes and looking satisfied, the leader raised his arms as if he were the conductor of a symphony and pointed to the next victim.

The man he pointed at tried to run away but was frozen mid-stride, arms up and one leg on the ground.

Only the sound of the female passengers sobbing could be heard in the lounge.

"That was a little early, but it was getting to be time at any rate." The leader turned back to Kakashi. "I really had intended to kill only one, but because of you, Hatake Kakashi, I ended up killing two."

"You…"

"I think you now understand, but the hostages already have a jutsu cast on them. If I felt like it, I could freeze every one of them all at once."

"If you do that," Kakashi glared at his opponent, "you lose your bargaining power."

"You do say the strangest things."

Kakashi gave him a puzzled look.

"Konoha doesn't negotiate with terrorists like us, yes? So then it shouldn't matter whether we have bargaining power or not. Konoha will not respond to negotiations." The leader grinned. "And when they don't, we will take everyone here with us, and the sightseeing tour will continue to the next world."

"Ngh!" Kakashi gritted his teeth.

"Take one of the hostages to the pilothouse and make them report to Konoha on what they saw just now," the leader ordered a subordinate before turning his back to Kakashi. "Hatake Kakashi, if you allow us to quietly capture you now, I can let the hostages live for the next ten minutes."

Kakashi's eyes flew open.

"However, if you go up against us, I will do what I have to do. I believe I've already proven that I am a man who does what needs to be done when the time comes."

The two exchanged looks.

This man would really do it. Kakashi felt it in his gut as he looked at the hands of his opponent, readied like claws. *If I move even a finger right now, this guy will definitely murder all the hostages.*

Sighing, he released the battle spirit cloaking his body.

Immediately, the attackers flew at him and tied Kakashi's hands behind his back. The ninjas he had taken down earlier got up and pounded his face. The corner of his eye where he was injured opened up, and blood dripped out.

It wouldn't end with just that.

The leader came around behind him and double-checked the rope binding him. In the next instant, an intense pain raced up the index finger of his right hand.

Crack!

He clearly heard the sound of the bone breaking.

"Ngah!" Reeling involuntarily, Kakashi was caught by the leader, who then easily broke the index finger of his left hand as well.

Snap!

"Ngah!"

"That's enough." He heard a satisfied voice from behind him. "Now you can't get out of these ropes."

Cold sweat pouring down his face, Kakashi collapsed to his knees.

"If you're going to kill anyone, kill me first!" Kakashi shouted over and over, but his enemy just snorted laughter at him.

"Your life is worth a hundred hostages. You might be useful in the negotiations with Konoha."

And thus, ten minutes later, Kakashi was forced to witness an execution once more.

This time it was a woman.

He could only watch helplessly as the woman, wearing a gorgeous black dress, was swallowed up by an inorganic glittering like the jewelry she had adorned herself with.

"Release Garyo or hostages continue to die! It's one or the other!" All the passengers pricked their ears up at the roar that reached them from the pilothouse. "Contact us within ten minutes! If you do not, we'll start killing them in pairs next! People will continue to die because of you, Konoha!"

Dammit. Kakashi was filled with bitter regret.

Each minute and second dragged by. If they were at least at a lower altitude, he would still have a chance.

What am I going to do? His frustration was strong enough to wipe out the pain from his broken fingers. *What on earth can I—*

It was three minutes before the next execution when a small voice spoke directly into Kakashi's racing mind.

"Master Kakashi, can you hear me? Master Kakashi?"

For a moment, he was baffled.

"Master Kakashi? If you can hear me, please answer. You're on the Tobishachimaru, aren't you, Master—"

"I can hear you, Ino." He quickly understood that this was Ino's mind transmission jutsu. *"How did you know I'm aboard the Tobishachimaru?"*

"Lee told us."

Of course!

"Are you all right, Master Kakashi? They've captured you, yes?"

"You're connected with Guy too, right? I'm fine. What's more important is another execution is going to happen in three minutes."

"Please look up at the vent in the ceiling without catching their attention."

Kakashi did as he was told. From the shadow of the vent cover he had broken earlier, Guy popped his face out and raised his thumb.

"*Right now, Master Guy has the explosive tags you sent Pakkun and the others to collect,*" Ino's voice rang out in his head. "*Master Guy's going to attack the enemy leader. While he does, please lead the passengers to the storehouse, Master Kakashi. Lady Tsunade has confirmed with the Land of Waves that inside the large boxes in the storehouse are parachutes. Use those—*"

"No!" Kakashi said to Ino, and gave Guy in the vent a signal to stay back with his eyes. "Guy's in no condition—and there's an enemy mixed in amongst the passengers."

"*What!*"

"Is Sai there?"

"*Yes, he's standing by in Lady Tsunade's office.*"

"Put Sai on. He might be able to rescue the passengers with his Art of Cartoon Beast Mimicry."

"*Right away.*"

"And I want to know how the Ryuha Armed Alliance got onto this boat."

"*It appears they waylaid some passengers and took their places.*"

"They did? At any rate, I'll create a diversion and buy some time somehow. There's only a little time left before the next execution."

Ino's voice in his head disappeared.

When he sent his eyes up toward the vent in the ceiling, Guy grinned at him again and popped his thumb up.

Idiot! Kakashi pushed Guy back with his eyes. *Don't do anything stupid, Guy!*

Guy's face was yanked back into the darkness of the air vent at almost the same time the leader of the Ryuha Armed Alliance returned from the pilothouse, even his footsteps loud.

"Just about time!"

The passengers held their breath.

"If you're going to hate someone, hate Konohagakure, which has abandoned you all!" the leader said, loudly. "They value a single prisoner who has committed no crime over all of your lives!" And then he swaggered before the passengers like a tiger.

When the leader approached, they all closed their eyes and shrank into themselves. His arm was slowly raised.

"Such a pity, but next is you—"

Booom!

An explosion thundering out from the rear of the ship drowned out the rest of his words. The ship listed heavily, and the passengers tumbled to the floor, screaming. The attackers also lost their balance and were forced to grab on to something for support.

Piercing alarm bells began ringing.

"What?!" the leader cried. "What just happened?!"

"Fire in the stern!" a ninja shouted as she came running in from the pilothouse. "It looks like someone blew up the drive area!"

Did Guy do that? Kakashi's eyes darted back and forth. He was sure Guy had used the explosive tags Pakkun collected.

"You still have friends here?" The leader approached like an angry demon and grabbed hold of Kakashi by the hair. "What exactly did they do?"

"No idea." Kakashi glared coolly at his opponent. "But don't you think you'd better hurry up and put the fire out?"

"Hnnnngh."

"The buoyant air bladder is right above the engine area. If you dawdle here, it'll all go boom, you know."

But it was Kakashi who was thrown into confusion seeing the look that rose up on his opponent's face. All impatience and anger disappeared from that face. In fact, it took on an almost relaxed look, as if he were enjoying the situation.

An intense unease raced up Kakashi's spine.

When the alarms stopped, the passengers timidly got back up.

"The fire's been put out!" the ninja who went to check on the situation returned and announced. "Two of the propellers were knocked out, but there's no damage to the air bladder area. The hole opened up by the explosion's already been repaired. We should have no trouble continuing on our course!"

Kakashi couldn't keep his surprise off his face.

"There's no way, it's just too fast—that's what that look says." The leader looked at Kakashi and his frozen eyes and laughed with what sounded like real pleasure. "We anticipated Konoha ninja infiltrating this ship. Did you think we had not prepared for the eventuality?"

"Kahyo, huh?"

The sneer disappeared from his opponent's face.

"Is that your trump card?" Kakashi asked. "I know she's an Ice Style user. It was probably her ice that put out the fire and blocked up the hole from the explosion."

"Impressive. So you figured out that much, hm?"

"Before discovering your trump card, I felt a little awkward about showing you our cards, but..."

His enemy looked at him carefully.

"But I guess that won't do, hm?" Kakashi said, and turned

his eyes to the ceiling. "Look. Up there."

Reflected in his enemy's eyes as he looked up was Guy, already falling toward him through the air, axe kick readied.

Well, he did work out even on rainy and windy days, after all. Kakashi took in the figure of Guy, who had thrown himself into his training after he was released from the hospital.

Annoyed with his right leg, which wouldn't move like he wanted it to, Guy howled over and over in a place where no one could see him. He cried tears of bitter regret so many times.

But he never quit his training. Whenever Lee was with him, he smiled that "nice guy" smile and popped a thumb up.

"See, Lee? A leg's just one part of the body," Guy would declare resolutely. "You can't let your other parts, which are all healthy, go along with a bad leg. In particular, you can't let this sort of thing lead your spirit astray. Even if your right leg's no good, you've got your left. And if your left's bad too, well, you still have two arms."

I underestimated you a little, Guy.

"Enter the Leaf's Noble Gentleman!"

Whump!

Guy's axe kick exploded onto the crown of the enemy's head and shook the ship itself.

The power behind it was intense, enough to rip a large hole in the floor. If there hadn't been space beneath the floorboards for the pipes, the enemy's body would likely have been plunged through the bottom of the ship and knocked out into the sky.

In the darkness below the floor, the cut electrical wires shot off crackling sparks.

"Sorry to keep you waiting, Kakashi."

"Guy!"

"Ah! Owowowowow!"

A dense fog of debris rose up.

"And all you passengers." Appearing from the midst of this fog was Guy striking his "nice guy" pose—thumbs up, with a wink and a gleaming smile—despite the fact that he was crying from the pain in his leg. "Now that I, the Leaf's Noble Gentleman, have arrived, you can all relax. I intend to get on the big ship and—Urp!"

Guy fell to all fours and vomited.

"Aah, your motion sickness is terrible too." A second after muttering this, Kakashi shouted, "Guy! Behind you!"

"What?"

Abruptly pulling himself up, Guy was suddenly sending a headbutt straight for the face of the ninja coming at him from behind.

The attacker went flying.

"Huh?" Looking at the fallen enemy, Guy forgot the pain in his leg and stared blankly. "What happened to that guy?"

But this one blow held up the movements of the other shinobi. They drew their swords and surrounded Guy, but no longer carelessly tried to close the distance between them.

"J-j-just as plaaaaanned!" Hopping around on one foot, Guy placed his hands on his hips and thrust out his chest. "Did you see that, everyone? This is the true power of the shinobi of Konoha! Nothing is impossible with the power of youth!"

"With a face that pale, you're clearly lying. Anyway, hurry up and cut these ropes for me."

"Roger!"

Wham!

The floorboards in front of Guy exploded as he took a step toward Kakashi. An enormous fist shot up from beneath the floor.

Guy jumped back, and Kakashi's vision was blocked by dust and debris once more. Wood chips danced up, scattered, and fell on him.

"Lord Rahyo!" A cry rose up from amongst the attackers. "You're all right, Lord Rahyo!"

"Rahyo." It was their leader striding forth from the cloud of debris. "That is the name of the one who will bury you."

Special Attack! Fists of Seasickness

CHAPTER **6**

Special Attack!
Fists of Seasickness

"Hey! You!" Guy barked. "I'm not happy here, you know!"

Rahyo looked him over.

"Might Guy here knows only toooo well how you're feeling. No matter how hard you work, someone always comes along from the side and snatches up the juicy bits. And on top of that, the guy who does it ends up being called a genius." Guy glanced at Kakashi meaningfully, and further insisted, "But look at me! I can only use one leg, but I don't go to pieces over a thing like that! You keep trying and work hard to develop the skills you can, you'll be able to stand up on your own two feet again like me. And then one day those stinking geniuses'll come to me looking for help. This guy here's a great example!" He snapped a finger out at Kakashi.

"You, seriously... At a time like this, what—"

"Now, Rahyo, my friend, you need to stop all this right away. You can't keep adding crime to crime. Don't hate the world. You can't hate—" Guy getting drunk on his own words was the same old same old, but even in a tense time like this, he managed to get carried away, and hot tears poured endlessly down his face. "No, tell me about your hate. Might Guy here will stop it for you with the Full Power of Youth!"

The passengers were already fleeing to one corner.

"Well, I suppose I'll have you stop it then." Crouching, Rahyo quickly wove a sign. "Ice Style! Ice-Breaking Sledgehammer!"

"Guy, this is no time for you to be drunk on yourself!" Kakashi shouted. "It's coming!"

Instantly closing the distance between them, Rahyo's fist plunged right into the guts of Guy, who wasn't quite fast enough.

His eyes flew open.

The corner of Rahyo's mouth pulled up into a sneer.

But the next instant, Guy's body, supposedly pierced by the enemy's fist, flickered like a mirage and disappeared. Guy's real body was already launching a roundhouse kick from behind.

"Konoha Whirlwind!"

"What?!" Rahyo immediately yanked his body back and launched his next punch. "Ice-Breaking Fist!"

Guy's kick and Rahyo's iron fist slammed up against each other.

Crack!

A light flared up at the collision, and the walls of the cabin shook fiercely. The pair leapt back at the same time.

Kakashi held his breath and watched the battle.

"Aaah! Owowowow!" Guy bounced around, clutching the leg in the cast. "Ngh ngh ngh! W-why, something so trivial... Nothing is impossible with the power of youth!"

"You know," said Rahyo. "That leg looks pretty bad."

"Even if my leg is broken, my spirit is not."

"In that case, I'll snap that spirit of yours in half as well."

"T-talk all you want, but it's futile." Guy steeled himself, even as cold sweat poured down his face from the pain in his leg. "Now! Come!"

"You can't stop us!" Rahyo yelled. "I'll take this one out."

Rahyo's arms, now the color of lead, had already turned to steel. Even from where Kakashi was, he could feel the incredible amount of chakra collected in those arms—an ice-breaking hammer that would crush a block of ice. If he took a hit from those, even Guy would be helplessly knocked down.

Guy waved his own arms, and almost by magic the Twin Fangs—Guy's specialized nunchaku—appeared. "No one's ever managed to slip past the Twin Fangs here and land a blow." As if to prove it, he began to spin the Twin Fangs so quickly they could no longer be seen.

The pair of humming nunchaku coiled about Guy's body as they sliced through the air. They were almost a living creature, almost a part of Guy's own body. *Shf! Shf! Shf! Shf!* Guy easily made them dance around him, cutting along his sides, wrapping his head and torso, while Rahyo gazed upon the sight.

All right! You can do it! Kakashi thought. Rahyo was hesitating in the face of the speed of the Twin Fangs and of Guy's ability to manipulate them so effortlessly.

But no matter how easy he made it look, Guy was still Guy after all. He abruptly froze in place and stayed there.

A furrow rose up between Rahyo's brows. As did one on Kakashi's brow.

The lounge fell back into silence, and the next instant, vomit gushed endlessly from Guy's mouth. "Unnnh... Kakashi." Tears of anguish poured from Guy's eyes as he fixed them on Kakashi. "I-I feel terrible. And my leg hurts..."

He's getting it from all sides! Kakashi was dumbfounded. *He probably looked at the Twin Fangs he was spinning around and made his motion sickness even worse!*

"Nngggrah!" A vein popped up on Rahyo's forehead. "Playing the fool..." He took a firm step forward and threw a kick at Guy's bad leg.

Guy's face twisted up in pain.

Rahyo pounded forward, his ice-breaking fist aimed squarely at Guy's head. "Die!"

But luck was still on Guy's side, after all. His feet got tangled up because of the motion sickness, and the right leg that sprang up as he bent his body backward—the leg with the big, heavy cast—somehow caught Rahyo on the chin.

Thhwk!

Taking a hard kick that sent him flying, Rahyo simply blinked rapidly, unable to understand what had just happened.

But the person most surprised appeared to be Guy himself.

"D-did you see that... G-gotta name it..." He thought about as he hopped around on one foot. "Umm. A name. F-F-Fists of Seasickness!"

You do whatever you want, Kakashi couldn't help but think.

"E-enough messing around." Rahyo gritted his teeth hard and launched an attack like a conflagration.

Although Guy had indeed just come up with a new technique, the truth was he was in no condition to fight. On top of not being able to use one leg, his intense motion sickness was distorting the world before his eyes. The floor was twisted up like ribbon candy, and it was all he could do to stand. Occasionally, he crouched down and threw up.

So Kakashi thought it was simply coincidence that Guy dodged the next attack as it grazed his face.

But what happened twice happened thrice. In fact, it also happened four and then five times. Rahyo couldn't land a single blow on Guy—staggering, crouching, barfing, wobbling, eyes wide open, swaying, twisting his body.

This guy! Kakashi was surprised all over again. *He's really mastered the Fists of Seasickness!*

"You...just never stop." The attacks of the enraged Rahyo gradually grew erratic. Still, one out of every three times, his ice-breaking fist managed to graze Guy.

"Hey, Kakashi!"

The small voice called out just as Rahyo's fist mowed down the bar. Bottles fell to the floor and smashed.

Kakashi looked down and found that at some point, Pakkun had appeared by his side.

"We got all the explosive tags," Pakkun said. "I'm going to chew through your ropes now."

Even as Pakkun was struggling with the ropes binding Kakashi's hands, the battle between Guy and Rahyo continued.

Foot slipping on the spilled alcohol, Guy fell over rather spectacularly, and Rahyo brought his ice-breaking fist down on him without mercy. Guy rolled away, and Rahyo's fist, having lost its target, punched a hole in the floor.

Jumping back up, Guy tossed off a counterattack, but not only was his haphazardly thrown haymaker dodged completely, he accidentally ended up throwing himself into the arms of his enemy.

"It ends here!" Rahyo's eyes, sunk into their sockets, glittered sharply. "Ice-Breaking Fist!"

The iron punch caught Guy in the stomach.

Whud! The dull sound echoed through the room, and Guy's body floated up into the air. His eyes bulged and the air in his body shot out all at once.

Assured of victory, Rahyo grinned.

But it wasn't just air that came out of Guy's body.

"Urp!"

Before he knew it, the substance jetting forcefully from Guy's mouth was making direct contact with Rahyo's face.

"Aah! Sorry, sorry," Guy said, timidly. "I got a bit of that on you...looks like?"

"I-I'll kill you!" Rahyo howled, the sour stuff dripping from his face. "Ngaaaaah!"

A storm of blows in succession assaulted Guy. Kick, thrust, palm strike, elbow, knee, fist—almost as if it would not be enough unless he used every single technique he could to cause his opponent pain, Rahyo struck. And struck and struck.

"Guy!" Kakashi yanked hard to rip apart the ropes already nearly cut by Pakkun's teeth.

"Is our business here done, Kakashi?!"

"Thanks, Pakkun. Next time, I'll treat you all to some tasty meat!"

Grinning, Pakkun—*poof!*—was enveloped in white smoke and disappeared.

Kakashi kicked at the floor and flew up, while his chakra poured into his hands to release a crackling stroke of purple lightning. Fierce pain raced along his broken fingers, but that didn't matter.

Noticing something amiss, Rahyo turned bloodshot eyes toward Kakashi. "You?! How on earth—"

Kakashi leapt out from the shadow of the collapsing Guy. "Violet Bolt!"

His enemy couldn't react in time.

But he ended up not being able to strike with the whole

might of his purple lightning.

Shrrf!

At the sound ripping through the air, he reflexively dodged. A kunai shining with silver light tore open Kakashi's cheek.

The moment he landed, he fled with a backward somersault.

Thk! Thk! Thk! The kunai that came after him pierced the floor. The instant they plunged through the wood, they melted away and disappeared in the blink of an eye.

Those aren't kunai. Keeping low, Kakashi glared at the newcomer. *These are the same ice fangs that came after us in the air ducts!*

"Kahyo!" Rahyo shouted. "What are you doing?! You're not supposed to let yourself be seen!"

"If I hadn't launched those ice swords, he would have done you in, brother." The newcomer, in a white ninja costume and a mask with a hook pattern, turned back toward Kakashi. "It'd be a shame to kill you right away. Hatake Kakashi, you fight me now."

CHAPTER 7

Frozen Lightning

CHAPTER 7

Frozen Lightning

"Ice Style! Earth Chain Ice!" Kahyo wove her signs and struck the floor with the palm of her hand.

An ice crystal began to stretch out toward Kakashi like a snake. The crystal immediately became an enormous icicle and bared its fangs.

Kakashi reacted without a moment's delay. "Violet Bolt!" He slammed the palm of his hand onto the floor.

The pale-purple electric current was transmitted across the gallons of alcohol spilled on the floor to meet the ice fang dead on, popping and crackling the whole way.

Booooom!

The ice and lightning, colliding savagely, caused an explosion large enough to shake the entire ship. The passengers screamed.

Caught in the blast, the grand piano flew toward a child who was a little late to run. Sweeping up the boy and dancing away was none other than the man with a broken leg and the power of youth on full display: Guy.

The piano crashed into the wall, and the chandelier on the ceiling shuddered threateningly.

Returning the sobbing boy to his mother, Guy glared hard at Rahyo. "It's clear you lot don't understand when we tell you, hm?"

"Ha ha ha!" Rahyo laughed as he charged. "This just got interesting!"

Punch and punch, kick and kick—the battle between Guy and Rahyo was completely even; only the number of moves steadily increased. Ten hits, twenty, thirty, they slammed up against each other violently.

"You," Kakashi turned toward his own enemy. "Two months ago, you were guarding Garyo, right?"

"We don't think we can defeat you and Konoha."

Kakashi was silent.

"But even if we throw away our lives, our message will most definitely reach someone," Kahyo continued speaking quietly. "And then that someone will move next. Like this, our will is handed down."

"Garyo's just an idealist. And the problem with idealists is that they'll burn down the whole world for the sake of their ideals."

"A world like this—"

"Should be destroyed."

She said nothing.

"That's what you were going to say, wasn't it?" Kakashi narrowed his eyes. "Madara and a man who was a good friend of mine probably thought the same thing. But I believe the truth is that they loved this world more than anything." He could feel Kahyo's icy eyes below her mask. "Naruto told me you lost your child because of the Land of Waves?"

"What!"

"In that case, it's not hard to see why you'd be happy if the world ended," Kakashi said. "You do this shinobi thing, and at some point, you're going to come face to face with the deaths of everyone you love."

"Hakuhyo—my son did not lose his life in war!" she cried.

"Hakuhyo... Hakuhyo... was murdered by those Land of Waves bastards!"

"So you swore revenge against the Land of Waves?"

"Death as a shinobi is something the shinobi chooses!" Kahyo shouted. "The moment you become a shinobi, you are prepared to die. I... My brother and I didn't want Hakuhyo to live like that. We became rogue ninja and hid ourselves in the Land of Waves. We simply wished for a quiet life without war, a life without hurting anyone."

"You're wrong. As long as we're alive, we have to continue fighting," Kakashi told her. "It doesn't matter whether you're a shinobi or a regular person. Wielding a kunai or wielding banknotes, it's the same thing. The very fact of living itself means you're always fighting for your life."

"Aaaaah!" Kahyo cried out in a strange voice and rushed toward him. "What do you know?"

Kakashi coolly assessed the incoming attack. His enemy's fist cut through the air and was blocked; the follow-up kick split nothing more than Kakashi's afterimage.

"The death of a comrade and the death of a child who shares your blood are two entirely different things!"

Kakashi bent down to evade Kahyo's roundhouse kick.

"Grief over losing a comrade is healed by time at some point!"

He pushed up an elbow strike with a flat hand.

"How could someone like you understand the feelings of a parent whose child has been killed!"

Kakashi grabbed the fist that was launched at him. "Then why are you trying to take the lives of other people's children?"

The boy Guy had rescued earlier was looking at them with

fearful eyes.

"The people that you executed were someone's children," Kakashi said. "This grief of yours isn't going to disappear even if you do destroy the world."

"Aaaaaaah!" Shoving Kakashi aside, Kahyo slammed the palm of her hand down onto the floor. "Ice Style! Earth Chain Ice!"

An ice formation so enormous all the others that had come before it paled in comparison encircled Kahyo and spread out, like a ring of ice flowers Kahyo made bloom from her own frozen heart.

Kakashi was not the only one doing a backflip to escape the ice fangs; Rahyo and Guy dodged in the same way, while the passengers stumbled out of the way or slid along the floor.

The steadily growing ice petals pierced the ceiling, lifted the floorboards, and pushed into the walls of the ship with sharpened tips.

"Stop, Kahyo!" The shout came from Rahyo. "We're still over the ocean! You must endure it!"

Kahyo had completely lost herself, however, and her brother's voice did not reach her ears. Just the opposite—she radiated even more chakra, adding power to the ice flowers.

Rahyo was forced to leap over the icicles and ram his iron fist into Kahyo's stomach.

Thud!

Knocked unconscious, she collapsed in Rahyo's arms.

But he was a just a tenth of a second too late.

Wham!

The jutsu was released at the same time as Kahyo lost consciousness, but before the ice flower could vanish like mist, it opened an enormous hole in the ship's body.

Air travels from areas of high pressure toward areas of lower pressure—the thin atmosphere five thousand meters above the ground sucked out all of the air in the dining lounge with a roar. Passengers, too, were sucked one after another through the hole in the ship—along with plates and forks, knives, spoons, the wood chips and bottles of alcohol scattered and broken on the floor, and the various equipment brought on board for the sightseeing tour.

Most of its wires now cut, the chandelier was just barely hanging from the ceiling on the one wire it had left.

The screams of the passengers were drowned out by the roar of the wind.

Still holding Kahyo, Rahyo grabbed on to the nearest pillar and just managed to hang on against the wind pressure that threatened to carry him away.

"Ngah!" Guy's body floated in the air.

"Guy!" Kakashi threw himself forward to grab on to Guy's hand, but couldn't get a good grip because of his broken fingers. "Dammit!"

Still, somehow he managed to grab on to one of the power lines jutting out through a rip in the wall. He was about to be pulled outside the ship, still holding on to Guy.

"Aah!"

Kakashi and Guy were thrown about by the wind like a flag ripped in two—up, down, left, right, trading places with incredible speed, slamming into the ship countless times.

"Kakashi, let go!" Guy barked. "If you don't, you'll end up falling too!"

"D-don't fight me, Guy!"

"No! Let go! I'll be fine! From this trivial altitude, it's no big deal as long as I have the power of youth!"

"K-keep your sleep talk in your sleep."

The hand holding on to Guy had a broken finger, and the hand holding on to the power line did too.

No matter how tightly he tried to hold on, Kakashi couldn't do anything about the power line inching away from the palm of his hand.

"Master Kakashi? Can you hear me, Master Kakashi?"

He didn't have anything extra to answer Ino's call with.

In the corner of his eye, passengers plummeted to the ground. And that wasn't the only thing flitting by in the corner of his eye.

"We've secured the passengers our enemies had assaulted and kidnapped near the ceremony grounds."

Something like a white flower petal, the leaf of a tree blown about by the wind—

"Master Kakashi, can you hear me? The Land of Waves has just now notified Lady Tsunade of the information about the attackers."

When he saw the hook pattern on that surface, Kakashi realized it was Kahyo's mask. Even as he was being blown up practically horizontally, Kakashi tried to search out Kahyo somehow. Kahyo, out cold in Rahyo's arms farther back in the dining lounge. The long curly hair yanked up by the wind—

"Master Kakashi? The breakdown of the twelve people attacking from the Ryuha Armed Alliance is eleven men and one woman. Can you hear me, Master Kakashi? The victims were assaulted by eleven men and—"

"Hngh?!"

In that instant, everything disappeared.

The noise, the wind, even time.

The power line finally slipped from his hand, and the last thing Kakashi saw as he tumbled to the earth with Guy was—

"*—one woman.*"

The woman in the long blue dress.

Five Thousand Meters until the Edge of Death

CHAPTER **8**

Five Thousand Meters until the Edge of Death

Tossed out into the sky, Kakashi found the ship's passengers scattered around him, all similarly helpless as they fell toward the ground.

He locked eyes with Guy. Seeing the sharp nod he got in return, Kakashi suddenly understood that Guy too was braced for death again. They could have been the greatest ninja in the world, but there was still only one way things could end if they hit the ground from a height of five thousand meters.

Dammit… Closing his eyes, he saw Kahyo in that blue dress.

"The longer you all hesitate, the more victims there will be." She had said this with pleading eyes when they were hiding in the kitchen.

"How could someone like you understand the feelings of a parent whose child has been killed!" she had shouted with her whole body from beneath her mask.

What could I have done? Could I have done something to her? The ridiculousness of it suddenly hit him. *Let it go. It's over already. Death will finally come. It's my turn to go there now, to that place where Obito and my father and all my comrades lost in battle have gone.*

Which is why when his body rebelled against gravity and floated upward gently, Kakashi couldn't understand what was happening.

"Good thing I made it in time." He opened his eyes to find Sai looking down at him, grinning. "Did you forget? You called me, didn't you, Master Kakashi?"

Kakashi sat up abruptly. He was on the back of a Chinese phoenix Sai had drawn. He looked around to both sides, and then up and down.

With the Tobishachimaru far above them in the sky, the Cartoon Beast Mimicry bird circled like a dark cloud. Guy, hanging from the bird's feet, grinned and popped his thumb up. He then lifted up his bad leg. On the back of his cast, the lone word "youth" was scrawled. The passengers who had been thrown out of the ship were clinging to the back of the bird or had been clasped in its beak, or even found themselves clutching its taloned feet for dear life.

"It's okay," Sai said. "I got all of them."

"Do you know the altitude right now?"

"Good question." Sai followed Kakashi's eyes up to the Tobishachimaru. "Roughly fifty-five hundred meters, six thousand meters maybe?"

Tobishachimaru's probably lighter now after losing all the furnishings from the dining lounge and these people, Kakashi thought. *No doubt it's drifted higher because of that.*

There hadn't been a cloud in the sky in the morning, but now, countless dark clouds were rolling in from the west. The air began to swell with the faint scent of water.

"Do you know who the attackers are?"

"No, although Lady Tsunade has a fairly good idea."

"The ringleader's a man named Rahyo." After hesitating a moment, he added, "And his younger sister, Kahyo."

Sai nodded.

Kakashi looked up at the ship drifting in the sky above. Its route was west by northwest. Was there something important in that direction? Kakashi put the gears of his brain into action.

The Ryuha Armed Alliance were demanding Garyo's release. They were using the hostages to try to fulfill that objective. However, they couldn't have thought that Konoha would simply hand over their leader. In which case, perhaps they had a Plan B in case negotiations broke down. And their trump card was Kahyo. There was no doubt about that.

He quickly reached the answer to his own questions. "They're heading toward Hozuki Castle. They had another strategy in the event Konoha wouldn't deal. They're going to rescue Garyo from above using the ship itself. We need to tighten security at the castle."

"What!"

They were going to pull Garyo up into the sky with Kahyo's jutsu. If she used the icicles of Earth Chain Ice, it was more than possible. Then all they would have to do was commandeer the Tobishachimaru and fly Garyo to any place he wanted.

"Ino," Kakashi called in his mind. *"Can you hear me, Ino?"*

"I can hear you." Her reply came right away. *"I'm so glad you're all right, Master Kakashi."*

"Tobishachimaru is heading toward Hozuki Castle."

"What?"

"They're probably planning an aerial assault—to rescue Garyo from the sky."

"Understood. I'll inform Lady Tsunade immediately."

"Sai?"

"Yes?"

"Take me back to the Tobishachimaru."

Sai didn't respond.

"I've got a bad feeling," Kakashi said. "And I can't leave the rest of the hostages to fend for themselves."

Riding upward air currents, Sai's bird broke through the rain clouds and, in the blink of an eye, came out the other side next to the Tobishachimaru. The hole in the ship's body was already closed over. The ice created with Kahyo's Earth Chain Ice bulged out from the sealed gap, threatening to overflow.

She was safe.

As he breathed a sigh of relief, Kakashi focused his mind.

The air was thin. Sai's estimate of around six thousand meters was probably on the nose. Kakashi did the calculations as he searched for a way into the ship. They could go up to around seven thousand meters and the passengers wouldn't pass out right away, even if the air inside the cabin wasn't pressurized to mimic a sea-level environment. But it was only a matter of time before they ran out of oxygen. And from what Kakashi could see, the Tobishachimaru was gradually ascending. Maybe the gauges in the pilothouse were broken. So the pilot wouldn't notice the ship's ascent—

"There." Sai pointed. "There's a hole in the gondola of the passenger cabin."

Kakashi turned his body in the direction Sai indicated. Through a break in the clouds rolling by, he scrutinized the entry point. On the lower part of the air bladder, at the base of the carp's pectoral fin, was a hole big enough for a single person to slip through.

"Good. I'll go in through that."

Sai nodded, and the bird tilted its wings to slide through the sky at an angle before stopping precisely beside the hole.

CHAPTER 9

Tsunade's Decision

Tsunade's Decision

In the Hokage's office in Konohagakure, Tsunade was giving orders and taking action like there were eight of her.

"Shizune, have we still heard nothing from the Land of Waves yet? According to Ino's report the leaders are a pair named Rahyo and Kahyo. Tell Waves that and get them to tell us whatever they know about them! Shikamaru, what's happening at Hozuki Castle? If they see any unrest among the prisoners, shut it down immediately! I don't care how! Sakura, put together a medical team and get over to Hozuki Castle right now! Shizune, put the Anbu on standby!"

She then closed her eyes and prayed silently. *"Ino, what's happening with Kakashi right now!"*

"According to Sai's report, he's slipped into the Tobishachimaru once more."

The office door opened with a bang, and Guy came flying in, leaning on Sai's shoulder. "Lady Tsunade! I, Might Guy, have returned this very—"

Konk!

Tsunade's iron fist came down squarely on Guy's head.

"Ooh... Aaaaah..."

"Guy, you—!" Tsunade grabbed Guy's collar and shook him roughly as he held his head and moaned. "You abandoned your position and boarded the Tobishachimaru!"

"No, uh, that's—don't be absurd! Th-the truth is... um, the

truth is, you see… Oh! Right, right, my leg was not so great, you see. And my personal doctor is in the Land of Waves, so… Right right right right! And I happened to be on my way to the clinic when the Tobishachimaru—"

"You—! Enough with the lies."

"Lady Tsunade, this isn't the time for that!" Shizune grabbed Tsunade's arms from behind as she tightened her fist, about to deliver a second blow to Guy's head. "Lord Ohnoki from Iwagakure is on the wireless!"

"Th-that's right, Lady Tsunade!" Guy breathed a sigh of relief. "Right now, our first priority should be the Tobishachimaru!"

"Hnnngh. Guy, sketch the faces of our enemies for us." She then turned toward the wireless set up on her desk. "What is it, Tsuchikage?"

"So no hello then, Princess Tsunade?" The wireless spat out Ohnoki's voice. "Well, fine. What's important here is that thing floating in the sky above your land. Isn't that the ship the Land of Waves developed in utmost secrecy?"

Tsunade was at a loss for words.

"Come, come, we too are shinobi. Someone like yourself, Princess Tsunade, couldn't actually believe you could hide something that enormous?"

"So from Ishigakure…you can see it?"

"Not just Ishigakure. I expect the other nations have noticed too. They're just pretending they don't see it, out of respect for a comrade they fought alongside in the Fourth Great Ninja War. Since it seems that guarding that ship is Konoha's top secret mission."

"Trying to play both sides, old man?"

"I never dreamed myself it would be so large as that."

"I'm busy right now!" Tsunade roared. "Just have out with what you want already!"

"My, my, young people are so impatient." A sigh slipped out from the wireless. "Well then, I'll speak. A few days ago, some unfamiliar fellows showed up in the village of Rokoku and stocked up on a large quantity of blue fire powder."

"What?!"

"As you know, Rokoku is a village of chemists. The explosive power of the blue fire powder they create is several times greater than any explosive tag."

"What are you trying to say?"

"We chased it down. After all, if something like were to be brought into Ishigakure, it would be quite serious. Well, that aside, it does appear all that blue fire powder is stockpiled in the ship bobbing along up there."

"What!"

"The Land of Waves is trying to use that ship to disrupt the world of commercial transport and usher in a new era of trade." The Tsuchikage's voice started up again. "But, well—Princess Tsunade, there's always a dark side to any technological innovation. Someone comes up with an anesthetic, someone else turns it into a drug. Someone comes up with a cooking knife, someone else uses it to cut another person down—"

"Someone comes up with a flying ship, someone else uses it for aerial war, is that it?"

"The other ninja villages are quiet right now because they're carefully watching the path of that ship. If it hadn't turned its snout in the direction of Ishigakure, we'd have kept quiet ourselves."

Tsunade remained silent.

"Listen carefully, Princess Tsunade," Ohnoki said. "I don't intend to pry into what's happening on that ship right now. But, well, if that ship doesn't change course, if it flies into Ishigakure, I'll shoot it down."

If Kakashi's guess is right, Tobishachimaru is heading toward Hozuki Castle in Kusagakure, Tsunade thought. *And Hozuki Castle is on the border between Kusagakure and Ishigakure.*

"The ship is heading for Kusagakure." Tsunade glared at the wireless. "In the event that it passes Kusagakure, I will shoot it out of the sky myself."

Nervous tension filled the office.

"Hearing that sets my mind at ease," the Tsuchikage said, before cutting off the call. "Having a ship jam-packed with blue fire powder hovering overhead is not my most favorite of feelings."

Double-dealing old man. There's no way he's satisfied with just this, Tsunade thought as she stood in front of the now silent wireless. *He's probably setting something up on the border with Kusagakure right now.*

Guy, Sai, Sakura, Shizune, Kiba, Shino, the members of the Anbu—not one of them said a word.

Ksh. Ksh ksh. Ksh.

After letting the static echo for a long while, the wireless came back to life. "Hokage!" An irritated man's voice reverberated in the room. "Has Lord Garyo been released yet?!"

"...Rahyo?"

After a beat, Rahyo snorted in laughter. "We're already found out, are we?"

"Change direction, Rahyo," Tsunade insisted. "If you continue this way, the Tobishachimaru will be shot down. Even if

Konoha doesn't do it, the other villages will not stay silent. You still have time. Bring the ship back to the Land of Waves."

"I'll decide where the Tobishachimaru goes."

"Listen to me—"

"Shut up! Release Lord Garyo right now! In three minutes— if you don't give in to our demand after three minutes have passed, we will resume the executions!"

The wireless was disconnected violently with a loud *chak*.

Three minutes... Tsunade gritted her teeth tightly. *What on earth can Kakashi do alone in that amount of time? At any rate, we can't release Garyo. If we give in to ruffians like Rahyo, Konoha will lose its standing among the five great nations. Our economy will collapse, and the people of the village will starve.*

Dammit, what am I supposed to do here?

The office was enshrouded in a painful silence when a commotion came in from the outside.

"Hey! Look there!" Kiba called out, as he raced over to the window and pointed at the sky. "I can see the Tobishachimaru!"

Dark clouds had filled the sky without her noticing it. Below them, the enormous carp was slowly moving westward.

"W-what is that?!" the stunned villagers shouted in surprise as they looked up from their daily business out on the streets. "An enormous flying fish!"

"Sai." Tsunade set her chin down over her laced fingers and closed her eyes. "How long before the Tobishachimaru reaches Hozuki Castle?"

"There's a good tailwind up there," Sai said. "At this rate, in about twenty minutes."

"Lady Tsunade, are you serious?" Sakura put forward timidly. "About shooting down the Tobishachimaru? Even though

Master Kakashi is still inside?!"

A silence that seemed eternal settled over the room, only to be broken by the voice of Tsunade.

"Sai, stand by in the air!" Tsunade ordered, firmly, eyes popping open. "Have Ino communicate the Tsuchikage's words to Kakashi! And everyone head immediately for Hozuki Castle without Naruto noticing!" And then she said, "In the event that the Tobishachimaru does pass near Hozuki Castle—even if it is simply blown off course by the wind—shoot it down immediately!"

CHAPTER 10

Heart

CHAPTER **10**

Heart

When Ino told him about the Tsuchikage's intentions, Ka-kashi was crawling through the ventilation ducts. He was just a little ways away from the opening into the pilothouse.

"They're starting the executions again. In about two minutes."

But just as heavy a presence in Kakashi's heart as the recom-mencement of the executions was the existence of the stocks of blue fire powder in the ship.

Dammit, where exactly are they hiding blue fire powder?!

"Master Kakashi, please get out of that ship right away. Lady Tsu-nade is serious. If something happens, she truly intends to shoot down the Tobishachimaru."

"Thanks, Ino," Kakashi replied, as he crawled along through the duct. *"But I can't do that."*

"But—"

"The people still on this ship have someone somewhere worrying about them the way you're worrying about me."

Ino was silent.

"If I can simply cast aside those people so easily, then I won't be able to protect the people of the village when I'm Hokage."

Dropping out through the vent, Kakashi silently struck down the enemy on guard in the pilothouse with some fluid, quick work. The pilots both looked back, stunned.

"Shh!" Kakashi held his index finger up to his mouth. "I'm a shinobi from Konoha."

The pilots nodded. A sea of gray clouds spread out in the large window in front of them.

"Just stay calm and maintain this altitude as best you can. Even if the enemy tells you to descend, trick them somehow, but please make sure you keep this altitude."

Kakashi had a reason for this request.

If there really was blue fire powder on this ship, the enemy had probably procured it for the purpose of blowing up Hozuki Castle. The Ryuha Armed Alliance standing by on the ground would take advantage of the confusion the blast generated to rescue Garyo. And the powder would likely be dropped onto the castle from the sky above. So to improve their accuracy, they would have no choice but to lower the ship's altitude.

He heard a commotion from the direction of the dining lounge.

"Please help me!" a woman screamed. "My child—he's been asthmatic since birth!"

Killing the sound of his steps, Kakashi approached the lounge and hid in the shadow of a pillar.

"He was just so looking forward to riding on the Tobishachi-maru. Please! If you're going to execute someone, please execute me! In exchange, just please let my boy live!"

A woman—no doubt the boy's mother—held a gasping child in her arms. Looking closely, he saw that it was the boy Guy had rescued from being crushed by the piano.

When Kahyo made her hole in the ship, the air pressure in the cabin had dropped instantly, and the air had gotten thinner. Kakashi realized this was why the boy was experiencing an asthma attack.

He ran his eyes in every direction. It seemed that in the early confusion, a third of the passengers had been swept out of the ship. The twelve members of the enemy group were now down to seven. Eight, if the one he had knocked out in the pilothouse woke up.

"I lost his medicine in the commotion!" the mother pleaded, desperately. "Without it, he can't breathe! He'll die!"

But Rahyo merely looked down on mother and child with cold eyes devoid of any emotion.

"Please! Please! Somehow, please—"

"I can't land this ship for the sake of a single child. You're from the Land of Waves, yes?" Rahyo asked. "What do you do for a living?"

"M-my husband is a doctor—"

"A doctor!" His face lit up with a cruel glee. "My nephew, you see, was left to die by the doctors of the Land of Waves. The child of my younger sister standing beside you there."

Still holding her son as he gasped for air, the mother looked up at Kahyo with eyes spilling over with tears. The other woman turned her face down.

"This is poetic justice," Rahyo said, and shrugged his shoulders with a laugh. "This time, it's our turn to leave your child to die."

Listening to the laughter that made his ears ache, Kakashi narrowed his eyes to focus on Kahyo. She didn't move. Her long, curly hair cast deeps shadows on her now maskless face.

Before he stepped forward from behind the pillar, Kakashi confirmed that the shadow of the bird was indeed floating outside the window. "Help that child."

"Hatake Kakashi?!" Murderous bloodlust immediately surged in Rahyo's veins. "You don't know when to give up—"

"Kahyo." Kakashi ignored him. "You said so to me before. That I couldn't understand the feelings of a parent whose child had been killed. But you do."

Kahyo's body stiffened and froze.

"I'm begging you, help that boy."

"You fool!" Rahyo roared. "This time, I'm definitely going to send you to the afterlife!"

"Shut up."

Under the pressure of Kakashi's gaze, Rahyo froze.

"You don't need to land the ship." He turned his eyes back to Kahyo. "A comrade of mine is flying along and following this ship. All you have to do is give the child to him. In exchange, you can execute me."

Kahyo glared at him from beneath her long hair.

"In that case, you die first," Rahyo interjected again from the side. "There's no guarantee you won't have a change of heart the instant we release the kid."

The attackers laughed vulgar guffaws.

Kakashi didn't hesitate. Instantly, he gathered his chakra in his right hand and chopped at his own neck with a striking hand crackling with bands of purple electricity.

Rahyo gasped and held his breath.

But the person most surprised was Kakashi himself. He had indeed activated Violet Bolt. And yet his strike only slapped up against his neck—no blood came gushing out, his head had not been torn off.

His right hand, which had been white hot, quickly cooled. Plumes of chilly white air rose up from his feet, and a pain like ice needles scraping against the insides of his veins raced over his entire body. Ice began to crawl up from his feet, crackling as it climbed.

Kakashi immediately sent chakra whirling through his body. The ice—which had already climbed as far as his knees—abruptly vanished like mist.

"There's no need for you to die," Kahyo said, softly. "I'll help the child."

"Oi! Kahyo, you can't just—"

"Be quiet, brother!"

"What!"

"Indiscriminate slaughter is not our objective." Brushing aside her brother's interruption, Kahyo looked into Kakashi's eyes. "And you can no longer do anything, anyway."

"When?" Kakashi asked, carefully molding his chakra. "When did you cast your jutsu on me?"

"The first time we met."

So that time I caught her when she tripped—Kahyo running along to board the Tobishachimaru, lifting the hem of her blue dress—I was already stuck with this jutsu?

Kahyo approached the child, nodded at the mother, and picked the boy up.

In that moment, Kakashi saw the sad face of Kahyo in profile, looking at the gasping boy as though it were her own child in her arms.

With a wave of her arm, a fissure big enough for a single person to slip through opened up smoothly in the ice plugging the hole in the ship. The air pressure within the cabin was already the same as it was outside the ship, so no one was sucked out through the hole this time.

Sai appeared with a cold wind on the back of his Cartoon

Mimicry bird. Bracing himself so that he was ready to attack at any moment, he brought the bird up alongside the fissure in the ice.

Holding the boy out, Kahyo said, "The next time I see you, I will kill the hostages."

Sai met her gaze with a blank face before leaning forward and silently accepting the boy.

Looking back, Kahyo said to the mother, "Come. You too."

Face wet with tears, the mother thanked her over and over as she took Sai's hand and became a person outside the ship.

"Th-that's not fair!" Grumbles of discontent slipped out from amongst the people remaining in the lounge.

"Why does that family get special treatment? If that's how hostage situations work, I should've brought along my own sick son!" said one man.

Closing the fissure in the ice, Kahyo waved her arm again without even looking in the man's direction. "It seems it's execution time."

Ice crackled as it swallowed up the complaining man, starting at his feet. After that, no one made a move to open their mouths.

"I activated the Earth Chain Ice I cast on you," Kahyo said, turning toward Kakashi. "If you don't want to be frozen, the only thing you can do is keep molding your chakra and sending that heat around your body."

"I see. So people who can't manipulate their chakra end up frozen right away, huh?"

"As long as you are using your chakra to suppress the Earth Chain Ice, you won't be able to use it for any other jutsu.

In other words, Hatake Kakashi," she paused, "you are just a regular person now."

"So it was you. The one who froze everyone other than Rahyo, it was you."

"I'm the only one who can use Earth Chain Ice."

"Why didn't you activate it on me until now?"

After a moment's hesitation, words tumbled one after another from Kahyo's lips. Her voice was stained with agony and pain and sadness.

"You said it before, Hatake Kakashi. You said, 'The very fact of living itself means you're always fighting for your life.' But there are some who are not allowed to participate in that battle.

"The village of Kirigakure, which we fled, was like that.

"It's not well known, but there's been a kind of class system in Kirigakure since olden times. At the top, those people from families whose ancestors, and their ancestors, were born and raised in Kirigakure. Next, those people from families who allied with Kirigakure in the long history of war. And then at the very bottom are families who fell to Kirigakure and had no choice but to be swallowed up by them.

"In Konoha, any mission accepted is given out according to the actual abilities of the shinobi. Not so in Kirigakure, however. The most dangerous and dirty work is always passed along to those of us in the very lowest social class. It has nothing to do with ability.

"From the village's perspective, we are so-called dangerous elements, liable to betray Kirigakure at any time. So we are assigned dangerous missions.

"We can do nothing but successfully complete our mission. But it's also fine if our mission ends unsuccessfully and we lose our lives, never to return home.

"With the current Mizukage, the situation seems to have gotten much better, but at the very least, this is how it was in our time. There were rumors among us that the former Mizukage was being controlled by Madara. At any rate, many people find their love for Kirigakure exhausted and abandon the village.

"I'm sure you've heard the name Zabuza Momochi. The man they called the demon of Kirigakure. He is one of the people who got out of the village as soon as he could. I heard he was such a gentle boy when he was a child.

"Did you know? In the past, Kirigakure was called the 'village of bloody mist.' In order to become ninja, we had to pass a certain test: students at the academy were forced to kill one another.

"You probably already know all this. But what you don't know is that the only ones forced to take this test were us, the shinobi in the lowest class. In this graduation exam, Zabuza Momochi, who was still a child, slaughtered over a hundred would-be ninjas.

"And that's where it comes from, you see? Calling him a demon. After that, he became a rogue ninja. In order to survive, he would cut people down for money. In the end, I heard he was caught off guard by some oaf somewhere and died.

"My husband tried to learn from Zabuza Momochi's failure. Better to leave the village. We could stay there, but people like us had no future. The homeless ninja tried to make the Land of Waves a place where they wouldn't have trouble in their lives, a place where they could live.

"As you know, there is no hidden village in the Land of Waves.

"That's what caught my husband's eye. The fact that there was no hidden village didn't mean that they had no need of ninja. He thought that if we could get the work the Land of Waves was asking the five great shinobi nations to do, then rogue ninja could live like ordinary people there.

"Only half of my husband's guess was right.

"That lot in the Land of Waves did end up requesting work from us. Thanks to that, we were able to make a living. But no one respected a group of rogue ninja carrying out dirty work.

"It gradually ate away at my husband. Yes, just like it did Momochi Zabuza. How he differed from Momochi Zabuza was in the fact that he didn't direct his anger outward, but rather inward toward himself.

"My husband started to drown himself in alcohol. From here, it's the usual story. He drank and drank and drank. Until finally, one night, he fell into the sea and drowned.

"With my husband's death, I left the village of rogue ninja. Carrying my young son, I tried to live somehow as a person of the Land of Waves. I did a number of jobs. All the work was boring, but it was the kind of work where no one got hurt; I was satisfied. We were poor, but I thought I had managed to rebuild my life with my son.

"That's what I thought...

"My son Hakuhyo inherited my Kekkei Genkai.

"One day, when he was playing with a friend, that friend, likely just fooling around, threw a rock at a giant hornet's nest. The furious hornets attacked them. Hakuhyo's only thought was to save his friend, and he unleashed jutsu after jutsu, things he couldn't have been taught by anyone. He tried desperately to protect his friend.

"Hakuhyo produced the ice swords through the method written into his blood and protected his friend from the hornets. No matter how much he himself was stung, he tried to dispatch the hornets that came after his friend. Thanks to him, the friend managed to get through it with only a few stings. But Hakuhyo was stung all over.

"And what do you think happened after that?

"That friend abandoned Hakuhyo and ran off home by himself.

"When it grew dark and Hakuhyo still hadn't returned home, I went to this child's house in search of him. And they looked at me with eyes wide like they were seeing a monster. Now that they knew Hakuhyo was the child of a rogue ninja, they wouldn't let him play with their child. The mother told me as much to my face.

"Even still, I managed to ask where the children had been playing.

"The sun had set and the moon was high by the time I found Hakuhyo. He... My son had collapsed, alone in the woods. His entire body was swollen. His face so much so that he was almost unrecognizable. And yet he muttered with swollen lips in his delirium. 'You can't go throwing stones at giant hornets' nests... Hurry, run... Hurry, run... I'll hold off the hornets for you—' "

When Kahyo cut herself off, the dining lounge fell into a sudden silence.

Kakashi didn't know what he should say. *Not only have I not had a child, but I'm even thinking twice about becoming the Hokage, the father of Konohagakure. Coming from a guy like me, any words are nothing but hypocrisy.*

Kahyo's eyes were dry. To Kakashi, those dry eyes were

much sadder than any amount of tears that might have come from them. Kahyo's eyes, so empty it wrenched at the heart, were the eyes of someone who had seen unwanted ends play out on more than one occasion.

Then he remembered the last days of Momochi Zabuza.

That had been their first job as Team Seven. Naruto, Sakura, and Sasuke had all been there. It was supposed to have been an easy job—cast a protective jutsu to return the carpenter Tazuna safely to the Land of Waves. There, a man called Gato, the wealthy owner of a transport company, hired Zabuza and Haku as assassins.

Zabuza and Haku had been fearsome enemies, so strong that Sasuke had nearly died. And yet, that that would end up being the last act... Stabbed repeatedly in the pileup with Gato's little henchmen, Momochi Zabuza's last request was simply that they lay him to rest next to Haku.

That scene—Momochi Zabuza and Haku lying next to each other on the ground—was overlaid on the image of Kahyo at a complete loss, her dead son in her arms.

"Why didn't I activate the jutsu on you right away?" Kahyo's lips moved slightly. "Maybe I wanted you to stop us."

He said nothing.

"I suppose it's too late."

What can I do? Kakashi clenched his hands into fists so tight, his knuckles turned white. *What can I do to save this woman's heart?*

"That's enough talk of the old days," Rahyo ordered. "Lock this guy up somewhere!"

The shinobi grabbed hold of Kakashi.

Kahyo was no longer even looking in his direction.

CHAPTER 11

Tears of Ice

CHAPTER **11**

Tears of Ice

Kakashi was put into the pantry in the kitchen.

Two shinobi roughly kicked him in. The door locked behind him with a *klak*. They laughed like barking seals.

"Can't believe we actually caught *the* Hatake Kakashi!" one shouted through bursts of laughter.

The other called out in a strange voice, still laughing, "Whoo! Ryuha Armed Alliance is number one!"

The air pressure within the cabin had dropped, and they were clearly not getting enough oxygen. When the oxygen making it to the brain was insufficient, people could become abnormally exuberant.

"See, Kakashi! You don't get to lord yourself over us forever!" The two shinobi kicked and banged on the door. "We came prepared to die with this ship. Don't go underestimating us!"

Right, like these two were doing at that moment.

They were feeling triumphant, and next, they would lose the ability to concentrate or make proper judgments. Then their muscles would grow weak, they'd lose consciousness, and finally they'd drop into something like a coma, and in the worst case, death.

Which is why Kakashi decided it was sink-or-swim time; he'd have to pull a trick out of his hat. He waited for his enemies' judgment to become impaired.

Looking at the shelves lined with vegetables and meat, he

noticed glass bottles of milk. After a little thought, he decided he could use the milk. He took the cap off one bottle and drank the whole thing down. Then he grabbed another bottle and got as much of the contents into his mouth as he could.

Steeling himself, he spit out the milk in his mouth as loudly as he possibly could. He coughed dramatically as he poured more milk into his mouth and vomited it out. When he had done that three times, it got quiet outside the door, and he knew that his enemies were listening closely. Without a moment's delay, he bent his body into a sideways "V" and lay on the floor.

The little window on the top part of the door soon opened, and he saw two eyeballs rolling around.

"Hey. What's wrong?"

"Unnnh... Unnnnh..."

Pretending to cover his mouth, Kakashi stuck a finger deep into his throat and successfully threw up all the milk he had drunk only minutes earlier.

"W-what the—" The ninjas were stunned as they watched Kakashi vomiting up this white stuff. "Kakashi's throwing up!"

"M-my head...hurts," Kakashi said, brokenly, breathing heavily. "Th-the ship's going...up..."

"What, that all?"

"You...don't know...? The air's...so thin...the ship's proba-bly...more than eighteen thousand meters up..."

Of course, this was nonsense.

"So what?" But his enemies were flustered. "What's the al-titude got to do with you throwing up?"

"Y-you don't know? ...If we get up to nineteen thousand meters...the boiling point for blood...is the same temperature as the human body."

This was true.

"So? You expect us to do something?" But the enemy didn't quite get it. "No reason for throwing up, is it?"

"From how I see it...five more minutes."

The enemies exchanged looks.

"Five more minutes and...if we keep ascending like this...in five more minutes...we'll reach nineteen thousand meters," Kakashi said, weakly. "Our blood will...boil at body temperature... We'll all...die."

The panicked confusion in his enemies when they heard that last word was such that he almost wanted to apologize: Sorry for lying to you guys.

"W-w-what should we do?!" One clutched his head, while the other basically turned in circles. "W-we gotta tell Rahyo right awa—"

"You won't make it in time!" Kakashi cried. "Let me out of here... It's do or die. The only thing left to do is for me to use my jutsu to make a hole in the balloon and lower our altitude!"

"Th-that's—But you got hit with Kahyo's Earth Chain Ice and you can't manipulate your chakra, can—"

Here, Kakashi plunged a finger into his throat again and vomited more milk rather magnificently.

"Who do you think I am..." He pulled himself up, panting. "I'm Konoha's...Hatake Kakashi."

Kakashi had never before seen his own name have such an effect.

Both enemies nodded, unlocked the door, and rather admirably, even offered him a hand to help him stand up.

Kakashi's eyes glittered fiercely.

Thud!

Crack!

"Don't think too badly of me." A minute later, Kakashi had locked the two unconscious shinobi up in the pantry, slipped out of the kitchen, and was leaping down from the suspended scaffolding into the storehouse.

If he tried to summon Pakkun and the others again, he would freeze from his feet up the moment he changed the way he was manipulating his chakra. He would just have to hunt down the blue fire powder himself.

There was nothing particularly suspicious in the wooden boxes piled up in the storehouse; sake, foodstuffs, the parachute vests.

Blue fire powder exploded when it touched water. Normally, the user kept it separate from the water in some kind of partitioned container, one that would shatter upon impact, allowing the water and the blue fire powder to mix. But he couldn't see anything resembling such a container anywhere.

The bad feeling he had got worse.

If I were Rahyo, where would I hide blue fire powder?

He didn't even have to think about it. He looked up at the envelope of the airship. He could see the bottom of the air bladder that kept the Tobishachimaru afloat above the scaffolding hanging in midair.

If Rahyo was planning to ram the ship into Hozuki Castle, the most effective method would be to set the blue fire powder in that air bladder. For water, they could use Kahyo's ice. In the shock of the collision, the air bladder would catch fire, the ice would melt, and the blue fire powder would explode. Hozuki Castle would be buried under a storm of flame.

No, there's no way. Kakashi banished the ominous thought

from his mind. If they slam the ship into Hozuki Castle, then Garyo, the very person they were trying to rescue, might be caught up in the explosion and die.

Their comrades were standing by on the ground. Most likely, Rahyo was going to drop the blue fire powder on Hozuki Castle from the air and try to rescue Garyo while Shikamaru and the others were caught up in the confusion.

"Ino? Can you hear me Ino?"

"I can hear you, Master Kakashi."

"They're going to drop blue fire powder on Hozuki Castle."

"That's what Lady Tsunade told me."

"They're dropping it from up in the sky, so they'll need some kind of target. Keep close watch around the castle. There just might be someone sending up smoke signals or something."

"Understood."

And then the sound of footfalls coming down the ramp echoed throughout the empty storehouse.

Kakashi immediately hid himself behind a wooden box.

The two shinobi who appeared headed straight for another wooden box, as though it were marked with a symbol that only they understood, and lifted it up with a count of "One! Two! Heave!"

It was at that moment that the wind gusted up against them, and the ship listed heavily to one side.

One of the ninja dropped the box, and the one supporting the opposite side tore into him. "Be careful! You wanna die?!"

At the angry look, the one picking up the box again grew pale. Perhaps he wasn't able to concentrate because of the low oxygen.

The pair carefully lifted the box and started walked back

toward the dining lounge.

Kakashi immediately inspected the remaining boxes. It seemed that the attackers had carried off the box stuffed with parachute vests. Which made no sense.

Normally, he would jump back up to the scaffolding in the air with a single leap, but he couldn't use his chakra like he usually did at that moment, so he raced up the ramp and took the scaffolding back to the kitchen.

He started to climb up to the air duct, but changed his mind and instead approached the dining lounge on stealthy feet. He couldn't do much with his chakra, and if he were attacked by Kahyo's icicles in the duct, he'd be helpless.

Fortunately, the grand piano had been knocked on its side near the entrance connecting the kitchen and the dining lounge. Quickly jumping behind it, Kakashi assessed the situation.

Rahyo was near the entrance on the pilothouse side of the room, opening the wooden box the two ninja had carried away. Above his head, the angled chandelier swayed dangerously.

The passengers, herded by the attackers, were in a cluster by the ice blocking the hole. Kahyo was also there with them.

"The Ryuha Armed Alliance takes no pleasure in meaningless slaughter!" Rahyo declared. "We will now release the hostages!"

The passengers looked at each other in confusion, but when the shinobi handed them the parachute vests, a cheer rose up.

"I'm sorry." Kahyo helped the passengers put on the vests. "I know we can't be forgiven just because we released you, but... I'm truly sorry."

Outside the ship, the wind howled, and the Tobishachimaru shook and shuddered once more.

The ship plunged forward through the turbulence, but the passengers, hearts completely taken over by the relief at being released from this nightmare, didn't appear to even notice it. They scrambled among themselves for the vests.

"Do not panic!" Rahyo shouted. "There are enough parachutes for everyone!"

Strange, Kakashi's sixth sense called to him. *That Rahyo would release his hostages so simply as this.* But he could sense no evil intent from Kahyo gallantly assisting the passengers. She seemed to be sincerely apologetic toward them.

"Good, everyone has their parachute on, yes?" Rahyo said. "Once you jump, pull the cord on your vest. That will cause the parachute to open."

Kahyo waved one arm, and the ice blocking the hole in the ship melted away in the blink of an eye.

Wind and snow blew in from outside. There was a commotion among the passengers as they crouched down on the floor and reached out for something to hold on to. And then, with a hand from the attackers, they jumped out of the ship one at a time.

Kakashi didn't take his eyes off Rahyo, who was asking his underlings about the wind speed and the landing points of the passengers.

Why... Why would he let the hostages go now? Sending his eyes over to the window, Kakashi could see nothing but the gray rain clouds. And why would Rahyo be so concerned about the passengers' landing points?

I-it can't be! In a flash of insight, a fire began to spread within Kakashi. When they had carried the parachutes out of the storehouse, the attackers had carelessly dropped the wooden box. Their panicked countenances when they did came back to life before his eyes. It can't be. Rahyo's—

"No!" Before he could think, his body was moving. "You can't put on those vests!"

"Hatake Kakashi!" Rahyo's eyes grew wide as he watched Kakashi leap out from behind the piano. "Hnngh! How on earth did you—"

"The vests are filled with blue fire powder!" Kakashi yelled. "They'll explode when you hit the ground!"

Kahyo stared at Kakashi with saucerlike eyes, and then looked back at Rahyo before bringing her gaze back to rest on Kakashi.

"I-I can't get it off!" The passengers began to break down. "I can't get the vest off!"

"Ah ha ha ha!" Rahyo's laughing voice rang out. "You're too late! Do it!"

The ninja grabbed on to passengers running about trying to escape and threw them one after another out of the ship.

Listening to the screams as they fell and disappeared from view, Rahyo glared at Kakashi. "If you and your people had just released Lord Garyo right away, I wouldn't have had to do something like this. All of this is Konoha's fault!"

A fierce rage erupted inside Kakashi, and before he knew it, he was flying at his opponent.

"Ice Style! Ice Smashing Hammer!" Rahyo's instantly hardened fists swung out to welcome Kakashi.

Darting quickly from side to side, Kakashi thrust kunai at his opponent, but given that he couldn't currently mold his chakra, the speed of the kunai didn't amount to much.

Carefully watching the tips of those kunai, Rahyo opened

his body and launched iron fists at Kakashi's stomach.

"Hngah!" All the air was knocked from Kakashi's body. And Rahyo's kick sent him flying to the other side of the lounge.

He immediately got himself back on his feet and commenced his next attack. "Violet Bolt!" Heedless of the fact that his body would freeze up, he activated the jutsu.

"What!" Rahyo faltered.

The thunder became a sword and raced along the floor. Instantly, he dispersed his chakra throughout his body to push back the mist that had already reached his waist.

Rahyo leapt back.

But Kakashi's target wasn't Rahyo.

The bolt of purple lightning hit the passengers and ripped open the parachute vests attached to their bodies.

It was a serious gamble for Kakashi. If his aim had been even the slightest bit off, the blue fire powder might have exploded.

But the fasteners on the vests bounced off and away, sending sparks fluttering in every direction. The passengers frantically pulled the vests off and threw them away, before falling all over themselves trying to put as much distance as possible between themselves and the hole.

Watching this out of the corner of his eye, Kakashi dropped to one knee, panting. Just molding his chakra the tiniest amount had completely exhausted him. Even if he decided to risk his life, one more blast of Violet Bolt was probably the limit.

"Seems that's all you've got?" Rahyo sneered, brandishing his fists at Kakashi. "It ends here!"

"Ngh!" Kakashi had no strength left in his legs with which to brace himself. He crossed his arms above his head and readied himself to meet his enemy's fists.

But there was no explosion of Rahyo's iron punch. His fist crackled as it was repelled by fangs of ice.

Kakashi was surprised, but his enemy seemed equally so.

"What are you doing, Kahyo?!" Rahyo roared with anger. "Why are you getting in my way?!"

"Is what he said true, brother?" Kahyo took in Rahyo with a gaze as cold as ice. "Those vests... Did you put blue fire powder in them?"

"C-calm down, Kahyo." Flustered, Rahyo became increasingly unsettled. "I-I'm sorry for not telling you. But it was to save Lord Garyo."

A lone tear spilled out of Kahyo's eye and trickled down her face.

Silence fell over the lounge, as if all sound had been sealed away within that single tear.

Kahyo's tear, spilling over and falling, froze in midair, hit the floor, and shattered like glass. Almost like seeds planted in the ground sprouting up, ice fangs grew up from the floor with a roar and assaulted Kakashi.

Kakashi immediately threw himself to one side and the sharp icicles brushed past him.

Kahyo cast the jutsu over and over in rapid succession. Ice fangs writhed and wriggled like snakes, tirelessly chasing him. When Kakashi kicked at a wall to push himself aside, the icicles smashed that wall. When he leapt up into the air, the icicles pierced the ceiling.

Concentrating his remaining chakra in his right hand, Kakashi sprang at Kahyo. "Violet Bolt!"

He realized something wasn't quite right when he went to hit Kahyo with Violet Bolt: His body was not frozen. As he realized this, he noticed that Kahyo had closed her eyes.

Two centimeters in front of Kahyo's face, the fight drained out of Kakashi's right hand, still discharging electricity.

"Why don't you hit me?"

"Why did you release your jutsu? You had to have attacked me on purpose." He paused. "Did you want me to kill you?"

As she slowly opened her eyes, he saw on Kahyo's face nothing of the severity of a shinobi, just the completely bewildered sadness from when he first met her, when she had pretended to trip and cast the jutsu on Kakashi.

"I've been thinking all this time...about what you said." He couldn't see her eyes hiding behind that long, curly hair, but her voice was trembling. "'When two rights clash, the most important thing is to risk your life and put yourself in your opponent's position.' What I was seeking was simply that. If, at that time, the people of the Land of Waves had been able to put themselves in the position of people like us for even a moment, perhaps my son wouldn't have had to die."

Kakashi said nothing.

"But, now, I-I'm doing the same thing as the people I hate the most. I—" But she did not get to tell this story to the end.

A random bout of turbulence caused the body of the Tobishachimaru to cant deeply to one side—which snapped the final wire, and the chandelier on the ceiling came crashing down on top of the box full of parachute vests.

Ka-boom!

The deafening roar of the explosion thundered around them, and the lounge was instantly engulfed in flames.

A large hole reaching from the bottom of the ship up its side spewed fire, and several of the attackers were thrown outside.

"Aaaaaaah!" It was no longer clear who was screaming.

And not only that.

The boundary between the air bladder and the passenger gondola splintered and ripped with an ominous sound, and just when he thought the floor was sinking, the dining lounge tilted and the ceiling broke open in a gaping hole.

"Everyone! To the stern!" Kakashi shouted. "This place isn't going to hold much longer!"

The passengers tumbled and fell on the inclined floor.

"Ice Style! Earth Chain Ice!"

Icicles stretched out and prevented them from being flung out through the burning hole.

The whistling wind fanned the flames. Those flames quickly became a pillar of fire, reaching up to the bottom of the air bladder. The spread of the crimson inferno was held in check by Kahyo's Earth Chain Ice. Cracking as it raced along, the ice covered the air bladder and did not allow the flames to eat into it.

"Just run straight this way!" Glancing back at Kahyo frantically weaving signs, Kakashi guided one passenger after another to the kitchen. "When you get past the kitchen, keep going to the stern!"

"It's too late!" The pilots came running and tumbling from the pilothouse. "The gondola's going to drop off!"

"This way!" Kakashi yanked on their hands, hit their backs, and shoved them toward the kitchen. "Hurry!"

Out of the corner of his eye, he saw Rahyo running toward him. But the floor sank down deeply, entangling Rahyo's feet. Beside him, the grand piano broke free and flew out of the ship, taking one of the attackers along with it.

"Come on, Rahyo!" Kakashi threw himself onto the floor

and stretched out a desperate hand. "Grab my hand!"

Rahyo blinked in surprise.

"Hurry!" he yelled. "This is no time for hesitation!"

Rahyo grabbed onto Kakashi's hand at the same time as the floor turned itself inside out. Rahyo's enormous body flew up into the air.

"Hng!" An intense pain ran through the hand clutching Rahyo, and Kakashi remembered rather belatedly that his fingers were broken.

He couldn't hold on.

Still, he gritted his teeth and held Rahyo fast.

"W-why..." Rahyo. "Why me, your enemy..."

"I-I understand how you all feel." Kakashi put everything he had into his arm. "But it's nonsense to think you can do anything and everything if your goal is a just one. If you're going to change the world, no matter what happens, no matter how hard it is, the only thing to do is keep being a just person yourself."

Rahyo opened his eyes wide in surprise.

"Brother!" Kahyo had somehow managed to put the fire out and was running up the now slanted floor.

But it was already too late.

When she flung her body forward and tried to grab on to her brother's arm, the bottom of the ship dropped out, accompanied by a collision like the ship was being shoved upward.

The incredible force ripped Rahyo from Kakashi's hand. As he was launched into the air, the look on Rahyo's face seemed to be asking how exactly they had gotten to this place.

"Brother!"

"Rahyo!"

There was nothing they could do. The force of gravity pulled everything down to the surface of the earth with its large hand.

"Hatake Kakashi." As he fell, the expression on Rahyo's face abruptly softened. "So there are shinobi like you in this world too."

Holding the sobbing Kahyo to his chest, Kakashi just barely managed to leap into the kitchen.

A second later, the gondola, torn in two, pulled away from the Tobishachimaru and fell to the ground.

CHAPTER 12

Human Bomb

CHAPTER **12**

Human Bomb

The flames enveloping the exploding Tobishachimaru lit up the sky over the courtyard of Hozuki Castle.

"Hey, we got trouble here!" Pointing at the sky, the prisoners shouted in unison. "That thing's gonna come right down on us?!"

Shikamaru had also quite clearly seen several parachutes abruptly opening up in the sky over Hozuki Castle a few minutes before that. Judging that Kakashi had successfully helped the passengers escape and that the falling people would need rescue, Shikamaru assigned Lee and Sai to the roof of the castle tower and ran out into the courtyard, with Sakura and Choji in tow, where the prisoners were milling about in confusion.

About the time Shikamaru had counted twenty-one parachutes, the Tobishachimaru was wrapped in a flash of light; the fire appeared to have been put out. But some of the parachutes of the people falling from the ship after the flash weren't opening up. And there was no mistaking the fact that the Tobishachimaru was out of control and deflating by the second.

Taking into consideration the direction of the wind high up, Shikamaru did the calculations. The possibility of the Tobishachimaru crashing into Hozuki Castle was exceedingly small. But—

"Seriously bad…"

Even as he sensed Choji's gaze on him, Shikamaru didn't take his eyes off of Tobishachimaru. "The gondola's fallen off.

Right now, it's like the ship's lost its ballast. It's going to just keep going up."

Choji gulped hard. "What do you mean, Shikamaru?"

"At about nineteen thousand meters, the temperature at which blood boils is the same as the human body," Shikamaru said. "Anyone left on what remains of the ship will die."

"What!"

"What should we do..." Sakura's face lost its color. "Master Kakashi is still in there?!"

"It's already that high up, even Sai can't do anything now," Shikamaru said, as though it hurt him to have to put the thought into words. "At any rate, we'll do what we can."

"The parachutes are coming down!" Tenten shouted from the watchtower. "Toward the tower!"

With the weak sunlight breaking through the rain clouds hitting the top of it, the first of the parachutes drifted and wobbled toward the castle tower. When Shikamaru looked up, Lee was nodding up on the castle tower.

A side wind blew in, and the parachute drifted away. The cords connecting the parachute and the person—the suspension lines—got tangled, causing the person's body to swing far to one side and then back again like a pendulum. The parachuter slipped out of the hands of Lee and the others waiting at the top of the tower and fell down toward the cell block.

"Kiba and Shino are on standby there—"

The landing point flashed white hot, and an explosion swallowed the rest of Shikamaru's words.

Boooooom!

The cell block was enveloped in white smoke, and flames were soon flickering upward.

"W-what?!"

"Shikamaru!" Ino's shrill cry hit Shikamaru's ears as he stood rooted to the spot. "The parachute vests contain blue fire powder!"

"Ah?"

"There was a message from Master Kakashi!" Pushing her face out of a window in the castle tower, Ino mustered up all the voice she had. "There's going to be an enemy assault!"

"Seriously...?"

The second parachute landed immediately outside the castle gates in a deafening explosion; the blast sent the castle gate flying. The prisoners looked at each other. They didn't know what was happening, but when the next explosion took down a wall, they cheered as if they had awoken from a dream and started running.

"Yahoooo! I can finally say sayonara to this filthy hole!"

"Keep 'em coming, parachutes! Smash this place to dust!"

The chaos didn't stop there.

"Lord Garyo!" Shinobi clad in black ninja uniforms surged into the castle, shouting loudly. "Where are you, Lord Garyo!"

"Tch. This just turned into a real hassle." In the eye of the raging storm, Shikamaru took aim at the shadow of a parachute falling to earth and launched his jutsu.

"Suffocating Darkness!"

Shikamaru's shadow hand stretched out, not to attack, but to save, and its dark fingers hooked on to the shadow of the parachute. With this as a support, he stopped the body attached to the parachute in midair.

"Tenten! Break the fasteners without damaging the vest!"

Leaping out from the watchtower, Tenten shot his ninja tools into the air. Once the fasteners were broken, the man suspended in midair slipped smoothly from the parachute and plunged to the ground.

"Aaaah!"

"Hngh!" Choji grabbed the falling man to stop him. "Hup!"

With the now-empty vest still attached, the parachute blew away on the wind.

Shikamaru didn't even have the chance to take a breath. The human bombs came falling out of the sky one after another.

"Shadow Pull!"

The shadow of Shikamaru's real-world body immediately developed countless tentacles and shot up to pin ten people in the air all at once. Normally, he used this technique to pull in physical objects, but he couldn't have these physical objects—namely, the parachutes—anywhere near him.

The sound of an explosion echoed from the direction of the castle tower.

"Garyo's getting away!" Tenten called, while breaking the fasteners on the vests. "What should we do, Shikamaru?!"

What should we do... With his jutsu activated, Shikamaru couldn't move. All he could do was watch out of the corner of his eye as Garyo escaped guarded by the ninjas in black. *Just what exactly are we supposed to do here?!*

Sai's large bird snatched up the people falling through the air, while Shino's Parasitic Insects became a black cloud and gathered up the parachutes. Some people fell after the insects chewed through the fasteners on their vests, and Lee jumped out to catch them in midair.

Kiba and Choji, along with members of the Anbu, went after the fleeing prisoners. At the same time, they launched Fang

Over Fang and Human Juggernaut to mow down prisoners.

In this vortex of confusion, Shikamaru looked up at the sky. Four parachutes remained.

"Shino!" Shikamaru shouted. "Can I leave the parachutes to you?!"

"Yeah!" Shino nodded, as she maneuvered the insects. "You go after Garyo."

Shikamaru's eyes caught the group in black beyond the throng of people. Garyo was being guarded by those shinobi on the other side of a curtain of fluttering colored maple leaves.

"Stop!"

Several people turned toward him and sent kunai flying.

"Get down!" Shikamaru dodged the kunai and wove signs as he ran. "Shadow Stitching!"

Shikamaru's shadow transformed into a sharp needle and stabbed into the feet of his targets. Blood flowing from their feet, the enemy shinobi staggered and fell. He continued his pursuit of Garyo, but came to a stop before he had taken more than a few more steps. "What the...?"

In a strange turn of events, his opponent was running toward him!

"W-what is the matter, Lord Garyo?!" The black-clad shinobi were just as bewildered. "Come! We must hurry!"

"Step aside!" Shaking free of the ninja, Garyo came toward Shikamaru, waving his arms wildly. "Shikamaruuu!"

"Huh?" Shikamaru furrowed his brow. Had Garyo always been so feminine? He pulled his arms in and stood on guard against the man running toward him like a little girl. "Stop right there!"

"Honestly, what are you talking about? I've got Garyo, so

you just go on and get the escaping prisoners with Choji and the others!"

He stared blankly.

"What are you just standing there for? It's me! You know!"

"Ohh. Ino?"

Apparently, Ino had slipped into Garyo with her mind-transmission jutsu.

"Listen up, you!" Ino—or rather Ino wearing Garyo—turned to the enemy shinobi. "You lay a single finger on me, and I'll kill your boss, got it?"

The ninjas took a step back.

"What are you doing, Shikamaru?! Go already!"

"Right… Got it."

Why he did such a thing, even he himself didn't know, but before he knew it, Shikamaru was gently patting Ino's—Garyo's—bottom.

"Eep!" Garyo—Ino wearing Garyo—bounced up into the air. "What are you doing?!"

"I've always wondered. So you still do say 'eep' even when you're like that, huh."

Ino—borrowing Garyo's iron fist—cracked down hard on Shikamaru's head with an Ino punch.

No one had yet noticed the three stars in the distance trailing along to the west of the total chaos of Hozuki Castle. For all intents and appearances, they were falling stars, but unlike normal falling stars, the three shining bodies were not falling from the sky, but steadily rising up into it.

CHAPTER 13

Stairway to Heaven

CHAPTER **13**

Stairway to Heaven

Kakashi held Kahyo to his chest to hide the sight of Rahyo plummeting from the Tobishachimaru. She beat at that chest in rage and grief over losing her brother. She buried her face in Kakashi's arms and wept freely.

Even after Kahyo's wailing turned to sobbing, Kakashi kept holding her to him. And then he said the thing that he had no choice but to say. "I don't want to say this at a time like this, but... the Tobishachimaru seems to be gradually ascending. If we keep going, we're all going to die."

He got no response.

"There are lives that can still be saved on this ship," Kakashi said, gently, as though trying to comfort a small child. "I don't know how well it'll go, but I intend to do whatever I can."

Face still buried in his chest, Kahyo murmured, "What will you do?"

"Put a hole in the air bladder."

Kahyo was silent.

"The old man who built this ship said that they used helium for buoyancy, which isn't flammable. So even if there is a fire, there won't be any big explosion or anything. If I can puncture the air bladder, we might be able to bring Tobishachimaru down for a landing."

"And if it doesn't go well?"

"Have you ever stuck a needle in a fully blown-up balloon?"

She breathed a tiny sigh.

"It's my first time breaking a balloon this enormous—" Kakashi stopped abruptly, and Kahyo lifted a face swollen with tears.

"What's wrong?"

He lifted a hand to forestall her question. *"What? Sorry, Ino, I can't hear you that well. You secured Garyo?"*

"We've taken care of it." Ino's voice sounded softly inside his head. *"Shikamaru and the others are still chasing the escaped prisoners, though. I've just had a message from Lady Tsunade. The Tsuchikage is heading your way. We can see him from here as well."*

Kakashi looked out at the sea of gray clouds swirling below his eyes through the gash in the gondola. Three shining bodies were approaching them at incredible speed.

"Mm-hmm, I can see them too," Kakashi replied in his head. *"They're going to shoot the Tobishachimaru down before it enters Ishigakure."*

In which case, making a hole in the air bladder would have exactly the wrong effect. Looking down on Ohnoki and the others closing in on them, he began racking his brain urgently. *The air leaking out from the hole will propel the ship—no, if I make the hole in the front of the air bladder, the force will work in the opposite direction and push the ship back, won't it...*

The wind toyed with Kahyo's long curls, and Kakashi realized once more that the wind was blowing from east to west. *That's no good. If I make a hole in the front of the air bladder...* He rethought the situation. The Tobishachimaru would end up going against the wind. If he handled it poorly, they would be thrown about by the air currents.

And if that happens, then we'll be battered every which way and

be bouncing around inside the ship long after we're dead. Like we got sucked into a washing machine or something.

The points of light slowed down and then stopped below them.

He thought it strange only for an instant; he quickly grasped the reason behind them stopping. The ship had gone beyond the range within which the Tsuchikage could fly and was still ascending further.

"Don't let them shoot this ship down."

"Yes, that won't happen."

"...What?"

"Please listen closely, Master Kakashi," Ino said. *"This is an order from Lady Tsunade. Please blow up the Tobishachimaru immediately."*

"Hold on a minute! There are still survivors on this ship."

"I understand," Ino said, without a hint of emotion before disconnecting the transmission. *"And Lady Tsunade understands this as well."*

Kakashi's eyes raced over to the people crouched down in the kitchen. Several had already collapsed and were greedily sucking at the thinning air, their mouths wide open. With the sudden temperature drop, all of them were shivering furiously.

"How high up are we right now?"

"Good question." A pilot holding her knees on the floor lifted her face and moved purple lips. "I don't have my gauges, so I can't say for sure, but... Given how thin this air is, I think we're long past thirteen thousand meters."

Thirteen thousand... Kakashi did some mental calculations. It hadn't yet been ten minutes since Tobishachimaru had been torn apart. They had originally been flying at an altitude of five thousand meters, but in the confusion earlier, they had to have gone higher than that. Assuming they had risen to seven thousand meters at that time, that meant they had ascended another six thousand meters in the span of ten minutes.

Six thousand meters in ten minutes. In other words, if they continued to ascend at this speed, in another ten minutes, the ship would reach an altitude of nineteen thousand meters.

And their blood would boil in their bodies.

No, that's not going to happen, Kakashi thought, desperately. *Before that, the air bladder will probably explode because of the pressure differential. In which case, it might be better to deliberately break the air bladder and lower our altitude. At the very least, we won't have to deal with something unexpected when the air bladder explodes abruptly.*

But if I pop the air bladder in these air currents, will I be able to maintain control of Tobishachimaru?

"What's that point of light?"

Kahyo's voice did not reach Kakashi at all. When she repeated the question, he finally returned to himself.

"The Tsuchikage of Ishigakure," he managed to reply. "He knows this ship is jammed with blue fire powder, and he plans to shoot it down before it enters Ishigakure. And not only that. The order I just got from Konoha... I have to blow this ship up."

"What!" Kahyo cried. "There are still passengers aboard!"

Kakashi lowered his gaze in anguish.

"I'm sorry. This is all our fault."

"I'm a shinobi. I'm prepared for death. But...the people riding on this ship, I'm sure they expected nothing more than a great deal of fun on a sightseeing trip. I can't believe it's come to this."

Kahyo bit her lip.

"Sorry," Kakashi continued. "I wasn't trying to reproach you."

"No." Kahyo shook her head. "It's only natural that you would."

"I-I've got nothing else up my sleeve."

"We just have to land the ship before we leave Kusagakure, right?" A do-or-die look colored Kahyo's face. "In that case, let's destroy the air bladder."

"We can't." Now it was Kakashi's turn to shake his head. "We make a hole in the air bladder, and the ship'll be buffeted every which way."

"I didn't say let's make a hole in it."

Kakashi let his confused expression speak for him.

"I said, let's destroy the air bladder."

He narrowed his eyes.

"We have no choice. We have to chance it," Kahyo said, large eyes shining with resolve. "I don't want anyone else to die."

∞

Just as he had been instructed by Kahyo, Kakashi headed toward the back of the ship, crossing the suspended scaffolding to make his way to the drive area he had used when he snuck on board in the first place.

The pilothouse had fallen away with much of the passenger gondola, so the propellers had stopped turning. He climbed the ladder and stepped out onto the scaffolding used by the crew during maintenance inspections. From there, the air bladder was so close he could touch it.

They had no choice.

If the Tobishachimaru kept ascending, everyone would die anyway. No—before that happened, the instant the wind carried them out of Kusagakure airspace, they'd face the Tsuchikage's attack. Or maybe flickering tongues of fire would spread all over and roast them all when the air bladder was damaged.

"Damned if you do, damned if you don't..."

The passengers had already been evacuated to the ship storehouse.

After taking a deep breath, Kakashi let out a battle cry and flung his chakra-infused kunai at the air bladder.

Skrrink!

The blade pierced the bladder, scattering sparks. A tiny crackling noise hit his ears, followed by helium forcefully jetting out.

And then, of course, the thing he had feared happened.

At first, it was a small red flame. A mere ten seconds later, it had burned up the back of the air bladder.

Whoooosh!

The external skin of the air bladder went up in flames all at once, the blaze howling as it sucked in air. In the blink of an eye, it had spread to the entire envelope area.

At the same time, the Tobishachimaru turned its nose toward the ground and started to fall.

Kakashi leapt down the ladder and raced back across the scaffolding. Above his head flames licked at the air bladder, and it gradually disappeared, as though God were taking an eraser to it, leaving nothing but the skeleton behind.

They began to lose altitude.

When he flew into the kitchen, Kahyo had already finished weaving her signs and activated her jutsu.

"Ice Style! Earth Chain Ice!"

Her voice was drowned out by the wind, but her jutsu was not. An enormous collision shuddered through the falling ship.

The Tobishachimaru sprang upward, followed by Kahyo dropping onto the flat slab she had made with the Earth Chain Ice. The impact knocked yet another piece of the gondola off.

Kahyo, still weaving signs, concentrated on her jutsu with a grim look on her face. The physical and mental burden was no doubt heavy—her arms trembled, her hair stood on end, and a trail of blood came from the corner of tightly pursed lips.

The chakra-cloaked ice surface gradually extended outward, as if it were growing up from the bottom of the ship, and the Tobishachimaru plunged its head into the sea of clouds, which parted and swallowed it up.

Each time air currents threatened to snatch up the ship, tentacles of ice forced it back on course.

"We'll land it." Kahyo pushed the words through clenched teeth. "I absolutely will not fail."

They were wrapped in a single shade of gray as they passed through the clouds; they could see nothing.

Their descent was so rapid, Kakashi's ears popped repeatedly from the changes in air pressure. Swallowing hard, he released the air blocking his ears, and the sound of the wind became clear again.

In less than a minute, the air bladder had been become essentially nothing more than its own frame. The structure left behind was black and smoking.

As if insisting there was still more for the conflagration to consume, the flames pressed ever forward. Above the heads of Kakashi and Kahyo were only the blue of the flames and the gray of the clouds.

Tobishachimaru broke through the clouds and continued its fall. It heaved from side to side, but each time, Kahyo created a wall of sorts with her icicles and kept the ship from sliding off the slab of ice.

The badly damaged ship steadily lost altitude.

And then Kakashi felt his body floating up gently.

He was indeed floating in midair. "What's happening?!"

"There's not enough water!" Kahyo shouted back. "There's not enough moisture in the air for me to make ice!"

Peeking down through the broken kitchen floor, he saw that the slab of ice Tobishachimaru had been riding on had disappeared without a trace. The yellow earth spread out in the distance below them: the mountains in full autumn foliage, the river glinting and glittering as it flowed.

Having lost its ice support, Tobishachimaru was falling more or less straight down.

He knew that they had broken five thousand meters when he saw the Tsuchikage flying up as though he had been waiting impatiently.

"Oi, Kakashi!" Ohnoki came alongside the Tobishachimaru, flanked by Kurotsuchi and Akatsuchi. "Seems this is the end of the ride! If it's just you two, we can save you. Woman, Kakashi, jump over!"

Kakashi and Kahyo exchanged glances. Kahyo nodded.

That was all.

With that, Kakashi knew she was of the same mind as he was.

"What are you doing?! You don't hurry it up, we'll have no choice to shoot you down with the ship—"

But Kakashi didn't have the leisure time to let the Tsuchikage finish speaking.

A surprised "Ah!" slipped out of Kahyo's mouth.

Almost as if he were about to charge the Tsuchikage,

Kakashi kicked at the broken floorboards and leapt out of the ship. His body danced in the air.

There was nothing but a few thousand meters of empty space between him and the ground. The wind ran fingers through his silver hair, and a hard determination like ice took up residence in his eyes.

"Good. Come!"

But Kakashi leapt over the reeling Ohnoki, kicked at Akatsuchi's head, and jumped even farther.

"W-what are you doing?!"

"Kakashi!" Kahyo shouted, not to be outdone by the Tsuchikage.

Kakashi concentrated the chakra of his entire body into his right arm. "I am going to make it rain!"

"Kakashi!"

"The rest is up to you, Kahyo!"

Pulling his right arm, shining dazzlingly white hot, far back, Kakashi beat at the rain clouds with every bit of Violet Bolt he could muster up.

"Aaaaaaah!"

Ka-booom!

At the incredible force, the clouds split, and for a moment, they caught a glimpse of blue sky. The force was such that Kakashi himself was almost sent flying by his own jutsu.

The Tsuchikage opened his eyes wide in surprise.

The lightning gushing out from every inch of Kakashi's body shot out in all directions and pierced the gray clouds.

Instantly, lightning called lightning. The rain clouds pulled together, electricity rippling through them.

"It's too dangerous, Lord Tsuchikage!" Akatsuchi cried.

"Hurry! Hide yourself in my shadow!"

"I don't need you to take care of me!" Ohnoki roared. "Honestly! Those Konoha ninjas, they go to absurd lengths..."

A bolt of lightning flashed out of clouds rumbling with angry thunder and split a large maple tree on the ground cleanly in two.

"Kurotsuchi! Help that idiot!"

Obeying the Tsuchikage's orders, Kurotsuchi immediately went chasing after an unconscious, falling Kakashi.

The first drop of rain hit her cheek.

It felt like he had been unconscious for hours, but Kakashi had only lost consciousness mere seconds earlier.

At the touch of the cool rain on his face, he lifted his eyelids slightly. The instant he did, a massive shadow jumped in front of his eyes. Startled, his eyelids snapped open, and Kakashi took in the figure of Kahyo desperately weaving signs inside the broken gondola.

The falling rain was called into her Earth Chain Ice and formed into ice crystals on the bottom of the Tobishachimaru, which itself was nothing more than wreckage now. The ice crystals stretching out from the bottom of the ship gradually grew into a silver platform that glittered in the sky.

And the Tobishachimaru glided along on top of it.

As soon as the ship had slid past it, the ice broke apart and danced off into space, glittering brightly. It looked almost as though the ship had become a comet.

If there were such a thing as a stairway to heaven... The thought came unbidden to Kakashi's mind as he watched the airship sliding downward, rumbling and roaring. *It would definitely be something like this.*

Bluish-white ice crystals drifted soundlessly, filling the sky.

"Looks like he's awake." He heard a voice near his ear. "What should I do, Pops?"

Kakashi was being carried on Kurotsuchi's shoulders.

"That boy was pretty serious about dying, it seems," the Tsuchikage said. "Got his reasons, I suppose. And that troublesome ship's not falling into our land, it seems. So we've got no business here now."

"Ah!" Akatsuchi cried out, wildly. "Something's flying up from Hozuki Castle."

Sai silently brought his large bird up alongside Kurotsuchi.

When the Tsuchikage nodded, Kurotsuchi tossed Kakashi over to the bird's back with a "Hup!"

"Tell Princess Tsunade not to grow complacent in her victory. It's getting to be time for us to hand things over to the next generation, after all." Leaving these words behind, Ohnoki flew off.

At that moment, for the first time, Kakashi realized they were getting quite close to the ground. He could see people squirming around like ants in the courtyard of Hozuki Castle, plumes of white smoke snaking up around them.

The Tobishachimaru slid down into the broad grassy plains surrounding the castle. In the field, the season for ground cherries past, thick clouds of dust danced up. The ship skidded across the grass, pitched forward, and stopped.

There was a commotion from the direction of the castle, and soon enough, a small figure came flying out of the gates and raced toward the Tobishachimaru. It was Sakura!

A pitched battle on the south side of the castle caught his attention. A whirlwind sprang to life and pulled the fleeing prisoners into it. It had to be Lee's Konoha Whirlwind. Meanwhile, the shadows stretching out and shrinking back in the courtyard told him that Shikamaru was holding firm there. A large ball beyond the courtyard mowed prisoners down—Choji's Human Juggernaut. And the two figures he spied tearing along the straight path from the castle were definitely Tsunade and Shizune.

Shino's insects, Tenten's ninja tools, Kiba and Akamaru—looking out at his comrades, Kakashi could do nothing to stop the heat that welled up in his heart.

Just like the Tsuchikage said. It's our time to start on this path.

It was then that a decisive change came over Kakashi.

Haven't I just been using the loss of the sharingan as an excuse to run away from the position of Hokage? he thought, abruptly.

Becoming Hokage means there are more people I need to protect. Which means I don't know when or where I'll have to face the same sadness as when I lost Obito. I was so convinced I wasn't ready to carry the burden of that sadness.

The people of this land, right now, even in this very moment, say nothing and support each other. They act like it's the most natural thing in the world, the same way they wake up when morning comes. Naruto, Lady Tsunade, Shikamaru, Ino, Guy, Lee, Tenten, Choji, Sakura, Sai, Hinata, Shizune, Iruka, Shino, Kiba—all of their faces came to life in Kakashi's heart one after another.

And from the bottom of that heart, he was proud of Konohagakure, of these comrades.

If those guys need me to, Kakashi thought, *I'll gather up all of their sadness and take it into myself. Right, like it's the most natural thing. And I'll struggle together with them and that sadness.*

That's what it means to be Hokage.

CHAPTER 14

First Order

CHAPTER 14

First Order

The rain finally stopped, and the dark clouds were swept away on the wind.

The chaos at Hozuki Castle began to settle, for the moment at least. The fires inside the castle were extinguished, and the prisoners who continued to try to escape with admirable persistence were gradually rounded up by the Anbu.

The wind gusted through the dry winter field, and the ninja of Konoha cautiously, carefully surrounded the remains of the Tobishachimaru, now on its side on the ground.

The air bladder envelope had been completely burned away. The skeletal frame supporting it had been smashed and scattered in the impact of the landing. Wood chips scattered and fell whenever a gust blew through the passenger gondola, which looked as though it had been ripped apart by a giant hand.

When the first human figure staggered out from the broken side, Tsunade's roar echoed across the plain. "Put both hands up and come out slowly!"

Taking that as their signal, Kiba, Choji, Shino, Lee, and Tenten carefully approached the ship. They couldn't say with certainty that the enemy wasn't mixed in with the passengers.

Sai was standing by in the sky above.

"Are you all right?" Sakura alone raced around among the passengers to check if they had sustained any injuries. "Is anyone injured?"

One after another, exhausted and haggard, the passengers came out of the ship. Many of them looked up at the sky in amazement, walking slowly, as if confirming that they were no longer trapped in that deadly sky with every step they took. Some of them collapsed the moment they set foot on solid ground.

When Tsunade nodded, the shinobi wrapped the passengers in blankets and gave them water. Sakura went around to treat those people who had broken bones or who were bleeding after the fall.

"Don't move!" Tsunade's eyes were squarely upon Kahyo. The ninja of Konoha immediately took up battle postures.

But Kahyo simply stood silently, motionless next to the damaged ship. Her large, bewildered eyes seemed to be searching for something as the wind played with her long, curly hair.

"You are Kahyo of the Ryuha Armed Alliance?"

Named by Tsunade, Kahyo nodded slightly.

"Do any of your comrades remain on board the ship?"

Kahyo slowly shook her head. No one could say whether that was an answer to Tsunade's question, whether it meant she didn't know, or if she was giving up and saying that none of that mattered anymore.

"You've done something quite outrageous. Because of you and your group, trust in Konoha has plummeted."

Kahyo maintained her silence.

"The Land of Waves has also completely abandoned the development of airships," Tsunade said, a barely contained hiss. "Did you think you could simply walk away from this?"

A gleam rose up in Kahyo's eyes, a readiness to fight, and she nodded.

"Get her out of here!" Tsunade waved an arm and loosed

her command. "Seize her and lock her up in prison until we get answers!"

"Please wait a moment, Lady Tsunade."

At the sound of this voice, Tsunade and all the other shinobi turned around together. An expression mixing surprise and relief colored Kahyo's face red.

There, leaning heavily on Shikamaru's shoulder, was Kakashi.

"Kakashi!" Tsunade cried. "Are you all right?"

"Lady Tsunade." He pulled himself away from Shikamaru and stood upright. "She—will you leave dealing with Kahyo to me, please?"

"What?"

Tsunade met his eyes briefly. "Do you have an idea?"

But rather than replying, Kakashi turned to face Kahyo. A breeze blew between them, kicking up an indescribable bittersweet sadness in him.

"Until just a minute ago, we were up there, huh?" he said, turning his head back up to the open and infinite sky. From between the remaining clouds painting the sky, a weak light had begun to shine through. "It's amazing we made it out alive." He brought his gaze back to Kahyo. "But not everyone was as lucky as we are."

Kahyo lowered her eyes.

"Eighteen of the fifty-seven passengers are dead," Kakashi continued. "And your comrades as well, other than you and the pair I locked up in the pantry, they're all dead. Do you have anything to say about that?"

Kahyo bit her lip and shook her head.

"Kahyo."

"...Yes."

171

"I'll announce your punishment, then. As a ringleader in the attack on Tobishachimaru, you—"

"Er." A voice from behind interrupted Kakashi. "Can I say something?"

When he looked back, a woman was standing there holding a child's hand. He narrowed his eyes.

"I...I'm the one you saved then." The woman bowed her head at Kahyo. "You released myself and my son, who was having an asthma attack, from that ship. Thanks to you, he was able to recover from the attack. I don't forgive you and your group for what you have done." She glanced over at Kakashi. "But I wanted to at least say a word of thanks. Thank you, thank you so much."

Kahyo lowered her eyes; her face was twisted in anguish.

The boy, now quite well, let go of his mother's hand and started running. Racing over to Kahyo, he looked up at her and smiled. "Thanks, Auntie."

Surprise flitted across her face.

"I was really scared." And then he added suddenly in a small voice, "But...it was kinda fun too."

As she watched the boy jog back over to his mother, Kahyo's eyes filled with tears.

"Kahyo," Kakashi called. "As the ringleader of the attack on Tobishachimaru, you must die. So many were sacrificed. This is the only fitting punishment."

"...Yes." Kahyo's voice was shaking, but it held a note of readiness to accept whatever came at her. "I humbly accept... any punishment."

"However, if you can prove that you are a person who could be useful to the five great ninja nations, I will reduce the sentence you face and make it life in prison."

"...What do you mean?"

"From where I sit, your Earth Chain Ice looks pretty useful."

She stared at him.

"What are you talking about, Kakashi?" Tsunade. "What on earth could you use her ninjutsu for?"

"Lady Tsunade." Kakashi looked over at her. "When it is cast on ordinary people, her Earth Chain Ice freezes them instantly. But ninja who can mold chakra can send that chakra around their bodies to generate heat and prevent their bodies from freezing. So if you're hit with Earth Chain Ice, you have to always be molding your chakra. In other words, the prisoners wouldn't be able to use it to escape. What do you think? Right now, there's no castle master at Hozuki Castle really guarding the prisoners. I think she's ideally suited to the role."

"I see." It was Shikamaru who replied. "The previous master Mui did use his Celestial Prison to ensure that prisoners would spontaneously combust if they molded their chakra. This woman's Earth Chain Ice would be as effective, but in the opposite way. Lady Tsunade, I think she might work. All the villages are exhausted from the Fourth Great Ninja War. Labor is short everywhere, so if we released everyone from this infinitely tiresome job of supervising the prison, maybe the esteem Konoha is held in would rise. And it would make a good example."

"Example?" Tsunade said. "What sort of example?"

"Well, it's the ultimate justice for Garyo. You know how he advocates controlling personal freedom?" Shikamaru shrugged lightly. "In that case, we'll just have this woman who believed in his way of thinking being in control of his freedom."

Tsunade carefully thought the idea through before nodding

slightly. "I leave this matter to you, Kakashi."

"Thank you, Lady Tsunade."

"But do the inauguration ceremony."

He stared down at his feet.

"This is your first job as the sixth Hokage." Tsunade grinned. "You can't possibly intend to refuse?"

Kakashi met her eyes squarely and nodded firmly. He then turned back to Kahyo.

"You said on the ship that the side with power is always the side that's right. If you become the master of Hozuki Castle, you'll be the one who's right. Show me your justice."

She merely looked at him, stunned.

"You will do it, right?"

"...Yes." Tears streamed from Kahyo's eyes. Hot tears that most certainly did not turn to ice as they rolled down her cheeks. "Th-thank you... Thank you..."

"Well then, I declare it as the sixth Hokage." His voice rang out. "Kahyo, you are now in custody of Hozuki Castle. The term is indefinite. At the same time as you reflect on your own actions, you will supervise the prisoners and work each day to ensure that not a single one escapes!"

Tsunade nodded, while the ninja looked at their new Hokage with pride.

"I'm not worried." Kakashi's gaze softened abruptly. "You are someone who understands the pain of others."

"I will devote myself...to meeting your expectations." Kahyo wiped away her tears. "If I can be of some use to you, Lord Kakashi...I will do whatever I can."

"Kakashi." Tsunade slipped a haori coat over his shoulders. "Mm, looks very good on you."

Kakashi twisted his neck to look at his own back.

Sixth Hokage

He pulled the profoundly weighty haori shut. Behind him, gentle smiles popped up on the faces of his fellow villagers.

A soft breeze blew through the burnt-out husk of the Tobishachimaru.

EPILOGUE

Dear Sixth Hokage

EPILOGUE

Dear Sixth Hokage

In the forest west of the village, Kakashi sat down at the base of an enormous maple tree. It was warm for March, and the sunlight pouring down from the leafy treetops above his head was enough to make him sweat.

He pulled a letter from his breast pocket. The instant he opened the envelope a faint, lovely scent wafted up to his nose, calling to mind that incident four months earlier—the day the Ryuha Armed Alliance attacked the Tobishachimaru.

He was a little amused by the coincidence. Only the day before, the five Kages had concluded a formal agreement regarding the management of Hozuki Castle.

After the crash landing and prisoner roundup, the Tsuchikage, Mizukage, Kazekage, and Raikage had gone to observe the castle. The Raikage said he wanted to see Kahyo's true power with his own eyes and had gone so far as to challenge her.

According to the people there to witness the scene, not only did the Raikage's iron fists dig out several new holes in the wall of the castle, but in a display unsuited to his age, he had even launched his Lariat. Naturally, no one thought the Raikage was putting his full strength into the fight. But even assuming he was only using half his strength, everyone to a person said that no ordinary ninja could fight as gracefully as Kahyo had.

She dodged the Raikage's attacks and dove at her opponent. And then, before the Raikage's face, she snapped her fingers.

That was all.

The Raikage's beard froze.

"Whawhawhat, when did you..."

"Excuse me, Lord Raikage." Kahyo smiled brightly before the Raikage's wide-open eyes. "I've ruined your wonderful beard."

The contest ended with no injury to either, although Raikage did lose the beard he was so proud of and was mercilessly laughed at behind closed doors by the people of Kumogakure.

The other Kages were entertained by the incident.

"I can just see the face of that spoiled brat, like a pigeon taking a shot from a peashooter," the Tsuchikage said. Or perhaps he didn't.

At any rate, after close scrutiny with their own eyes, the other Kages reached their conclusion. Kahyo's abilities were on par with those of her predecessor, Mui of Kusagakure, and given that there was no one as suited to becoming the new master of Hozuki Castle, they all supported the Sixth Hokage's command.

Kakashi opened the letter folded in four.

Dear Sixth Hokage,
I hope you have been well. I—

"All right!" Echoing out from within the woods was Guy's loud, stifling voice. "Today, we go again full throttle with youth power, Lee!"

"Yes, Master Guy!"

And then, pushed in his wheelchair by Lee—*fwsh fwsh*—he went back and forth several times.

"What's this?" Guy made a show of his surprise. "Why, if it isn't the sixth Hokage Hatake Kakashi sitting there."

Kakashi cringed.

"And that letter..." Guy pressed toward Lee's ear with a stage whisper. "That Kakashi, while I was off fighting to save the lives of the passengers during that thing on the Tobishachimaru, he was shamelessly carrying on with an enemy ninja woman."

"So what everyone in the village is saying is true then," Lee whispered, equally dramatic. "I won't grow up to be an adult like that, Master Guy."

"You two..." Kakashi folded the letter and slipped it into his pocket. "How many times do I have to tell you it's not like that with me and Kahyo?"

But Guy and Lee ignored Kakashi and began doing single-leg squats.

"I often said, my student!" Guy continued easy squats with his one leg. "Even if a man like that ends up Hokage, I still intend to properly advise him! Alllll right! Today is five thousand single-leg squats!"

"Yes, Master Guy!"

Kakashi stood up and quietly departed the scene.

The next time he tried to read the letter was in the storefront of the tea shop. He ordered a cup of matcha, and while he waited for it to be brought to him, he opened up the letter from Kahyo.

Dear Sixth Hokage,
I hope you have been well. I—

"Oh, Master Kakashi!"

Shifting his gaze, he saw Shikamaru and Choji make their way leisurely into the tea shop.

"What are you reading, Master Kakashi?" Choji asked, crunching away on potato chips. "Oh! Is it maybe a letter from that woman you abused your authority to make yours?"

"Make mine? Hold on a minute!" Kakashi hurriedly stuffed the letter into his pocket. "You still seem to have the wrong impression. That was my first job as Hokage. I definitely would not abuse my authority—"

"C'mon, don't go saying that, Choji," Shikamaru jumped in. "I mean, Master Kakashi's long past thirty. No big deal if he has a woman or two."

"No, I'm telling you—"

"That Kahyo person was pretty, after all." Choji. "Older, but still."

And then the two of them stared at Kakashi, grinning.

Kakashi paid for the tea without drinking it and put the shop behind him.

As he walked along the village's main street, villagers came one after another to say hello. Although once he had passed them, he could hear giggles and snickers.

This is weird, Kakashi thought, thoroughly self-conscious. *How does everyone know I got a letter from Kahyo?*

He walked a little farther and turned off onto a path with no one on it. He then looked both ways to confirm that there was no sign of his ridiculously persistent comrades, and yanked the letter from his pocket once more.

Dear Sixth Hokage,
I hope you have been well. I—

"Take a look at that."

"Grinning, indecent."

Turning in the direction of the voices, Kakashi spied the faces of Sakura, Ino, and Hinata peering out from above a wooden wall.

"Ah!" Kakashi was startled out of his wits, and the letter danced up from his hand. "Y-y-you—where did you come from!"

"Look, see how flustered he is," Ino said. "It's because he has impure thoughts that he's getting that flustered."

Sakura turned her eyes on him as though she were looking at something filthy.

"So the rumors are true then?" Hinata said. "Kahyo's chasing Master Kakashi in exchange for him giving her the post of master at Hozuki Castle?"

"O-o-of course the rumors are not true!" Kakashi yelled. "Who on earth is saying such baseless things?!"

But the girls weren't listening anymore. Whispering among themselves, they chirped and tweeted like three sparrows: "What? Really?" or "I can't believe it." or "That far already?"

Kakashi started walking again.

Apparently, the only place he could maintain his privacy was the office of the Hokage. He returned to the main street and trudging along, came up against a bit of a crowd. On the other side, someone was calling out in a high-pitched voice.

The people gathered there burst out laughing.

"I honestly saw it with these very eyes!" In the center of the circle was Naruto. "Master Kakashi writing a letter, ripping it up, writing a letter, ripping it up. I mean, that was totally a love letter! For real!"

Kakashi stared.

"Dunno if he's gonna be okay as the sixth Hokage like that!!"

Naruto raised his carefree voice. "Nah, I won't say he's in love, but, you know, it's a serious illness, you know. The other day, right, he picked a flower, okay? And he did the whole loves-me-loves-me-not thing, pulling the petals off one by one!"

"So it's you." Eyes glittering, Kakashi pulled himself to stand tall behind Naruto. "You're the one telling tales about a bunch of half-truths?"

"Huh?" When he turned around, a distinct shade of fear rose up in Naruto's eyes. "M-master Kakashi! W-wait, I can—"

Kunk!

"What on earth is this about? What are you doing?!" Kakashi brandished the fist he had dropped on Naruto's head. "I might not be so forgiving this time!"

"It's just, I mean..." With teary eyes, Naruto rubbed his head as he made his appeal. "I'm the only one left out here. Everyone else got to fight at Hozuki Castle. And I was just hanging out in the village when you were almost dying, Master Kakashi!"

"Naruto..."

Naruto rubbed his eyes.

"Sorry for hitting you," Kakashi said. "And we hid it from because you have to take care of this village for me if anything happens to me."

"I know that much. Geez."

"Aaah, this guy seriously can't take a joke." Shikamaru and Choji came over from the other side of the street. "This idiot's telling all his tall tales, but no one seriously believed any of it."

Choji nodded.

"That's right." From the opposite side of the street, Sakura and Ino came along with Hinata in tow. "We were all just teasing you a bit, Master Kakashi."

KAKASHI'S STORY

"Naruto, are you okay?" Hinata offered Naruto a hand and helped him to his feet. "Hitting him over a thing like this. Master Kakashi, that's terrible."

"What? But Naruto there—"

"Naruto's hurt," Shikamaru said. "You're the Hokage, you should know that much at least."

"Well, it's all fine and good to say that—"

"I think you should apologize, Master Kakashi," Sakura and Ino said, sharply. "It was just an innocent prank, after all!"

"Aah, fine!" Kakashi finally shouted. "I get it. I understand. What do I have to do for you to forgive me?"

Naruto and Shikamaru exchanged looks and grinned.

Dammit! The instant he saw that, Kakashi knew that he had fallen into a trap. *These kids got me!*

"To heal my damaged heart," Naruto said, "the only thing that works is ramen!"

"..."

Everyone there held their breath and waited for Kakashi's response.

"Fine, fine." Kakashi could only throw up both hands and assume a posture of surrender. "How about we all go grab some ramen right now?"

"Yay!" A cheer rose up. "All right!"

"Told you it'd work!"

Honestly... In his heart, Kakashi shook his head. Abruptly, the ridiculousness of it hit him. *I'm the Hokage now, but I still do the same things. Every day, I eat, I sleep, I worry about stupid things. My job is to make sure these kids have as many days as they can where they can be idiots like this.*

Right, that's it, isn't it...Obito?

And then he chased after his students gleefully headed to one of their favorite pastimes, the sun pouring down on them all.

Somewhere, a nightingale warbled.

Dear Sixth Hokage,

I hope you have been well. I am always pressed with the everyday business of work, but as the season shifts each day to spring, I carry out my duties with a peaceful heart…

Spring had indeed arrived.

FICTION

The adventures of your favorite ninja continue in exciting new novels!

— COMING **FEBRUARY 2016** —

NARUTO: SHIKAMARU'S STORY
by Masashi Kishimoto and Takashi Yano

SRP: $10.99 USA / $12.99 CA / £6.99 UK / $14.95 AUS
ISBN: 978-1-4215-8441-6
2/2/16, 180pp

Two years after the Great Ninja War, Shikamaru spends his days racing around, hands full as one of Konoha's key protectors. Then one day a large number of ninja from every region are reported missing. Even Sai disappears. And the place where the missing shinobi end up is the mysterious empire, the Land of Silence.

As a ninja, as an adult, to protect all that he is responsible for, Shikamaru must do battle with the shadow of a new generation.

— COMING **MAY 2016** —

NARUTO: SAKURA'S STORY

www.naruto.com